SIXGUNS IN A
BLOODY DAWN

Sixguns in a Bloody Dawn

Bradford Scott

WHEELER
CHIVERS

This Large Print edition is published by Wheeler Publishing, Waterville, Maine, USA and by AudioGO Ltd, Bath, England.
Wheeler Publishing, a part of Gale, Cengage Learning.
Copyright © 1968 by Leslie Scott.
A Walt Slade Western.
The moral right of the author has been asserted.

LIBRARY OF CONGRESS CATALOGING-IN-PUBLICATION DATA

Scott, Bradford, 1893–1975.
  Sixguns in a bloody dawn / by Bradford Scott.
    p. cm. — (Wheeler Publishing large print western) (A Walt
Slade western)
  ISBN-13: 978-1-4104-3201-8 (softcover)
  ISBN-10: 1-4104-3201-7 (softcover)
  1. Large type books. I. Title.
PS3537.C9265S559 2010
813'.52—dc22   2010030712

BRITISH LIBRARY CATALOGUING-IN-PUBLICATION DATA AVAILABLE
Published in 2010 in the U.S. by arrangement with Golden West Literary Agency.
Published in 2011 in the U.K. by arrangement with Golden West Literary Agency.

U.K. Hardcover: 978 1 408 49339 7 (Chivers Large Print)
U.K. Softcover: 978 1 408 49340 3 (Camden Large Print)

Printed in the United States of America
1 2 3 4 5 6 7 14 13 12 11 10

SIXGUNS IN A
BLOODY DAWN

1

"I can't believe it," said old Tom Calder, Sheriff of Cameron County, Texas. "You ride into town without shootin' anybody, don't run into a gunfight, or anything. Plumb peaceful. Been here nigh onto two hours with nothing happening. I just can't believe it's so."

"Don't hurry me," chuckled Ranger Walt Slade, named *El Halcón* — The Hawk — by the *peónes* of the Rio Grande villages. "Let me have the full two hours before passing judgment." The sheriff snorted and fetched cups of steaming coffee from the back room of his office, spiking his brew liberally from a bottle in the desk drawer. Slade took his straight. They sipped and smoked, each busy with his own thoughts.

Suddenly the two peace officers straightened in their chairs. From somewhere not far off came a crackle of gunfire. Then —
BOOM!

The window panes shivered! The ceiling beams creaked and groaned! The shingles ground together!

"I knew it!" bawled Calder. "Not here two hours and somebody blows up the town! What in blazes was it, and where was it?"

"Sounded like dynamite, and it was close," Slade replied. "Let's go see."

They hurried out. Men in the street were yelling and cursing, all running in one direction.

"It was the Cattleman's Hotel!" somebody shouted. "Somebody blew up the hotel."

"That's where you figured to stay tonight, ain't it?" the sheriff asked accusingly.

"I did register for a room there and put my pouches in it," Slade admitted. "Agosto, the stable keeper, has my saddle and rifle."

"Mighta knowed it!" growled Calder as they followed the crowd and soon reached the hotel, their boots crunching on fragments of glass scattered on the sidewalk. It seemed every window in the building was broken.

They entered the lobby, already jammed with an excited mob. The desk clerk, a salty oldtimer, was holding forth in answer to the questions the onlookers bombarded him with.

"Take it easy, Blaine, and tell us what the

devil did happen," the sheriff blared at him over the babble.

"I don't hardly know," replied the clerk. "I was checkin' the rooms and looked out a window and saw some hellion climbing that big tree in the back yard. Looked like he was packin' a bundle of something. I hollered at him and asked what the devil he was doing. He pulled a gun and took a shot at me, missed. I shot back a couple of times, then the whole place blew up. Knocked me clean across the room and into the hall."

"Would appear one of your slugs hit the bundle of dynamite the gentleman was carrying," Slade observed. "Come on, let's go back and see what's there."

As they rounded the corner of the building, from the gloom of the yard came a horrified yowl,

"Jumpin' Jehoshaphat! Here's a man's foot!"

"And here's an arm!" squalled another voice. "What in blazes?"

"Looks like we'll have difficulty assembling the dynamiter," Slade remarked. His great voice rolled in thunder through the tumult, stilling it for the moment:

"Quiet down, and fetch lamps, so we can see what *has* happened back here."

The lamps arrived quickly. Their warm

glow revealed a ghastly scene. The body of the dynamiter had been fearfully mangled. One foot was missing, one arm and a part of the shoulder to which it had been attached. The corpse had been neatly decapitated, the head lying a yard or so from what remained of the body.

Calder cocked an eye up the big tree the dynamiter had been climbing when killed, one stout branch of which brushed the wall of the building.

"See that limb that goes right under the window there?" he said to Slade. "Would be easy to step off the limb and through the window. Betcha that's the window of the room you signed up for."

"It is possible," Slade conceded. As a matter of fact, he knew very well it was the window of the room he'd registered for.

Calder turned to the desk clerk. "Blaine," he said, "I seem to rec'lect you have a stretcher in your closet. Have somebody fetch it and we'll round up what we can of that scrambled horned toad and pack it to the office for Doc Cooper to hold an inquest on, when he is of a mind to."

The stretcher was brought and willing volunteers helped collect the fragments of what had once been a man and bore them to the office in triumph.

"Blasted wind spider was up to no good and got just what was coming to him," was the consensus. "Wonder what he *was* up to, anyhow? Must have had a grudge against the hotel, or maybe somebody in it," remarked one of the stretcher bearers.

"Listen," said another, in low tones, "Don't you know that big tall feller with shoulders a yard wide who's with the sheriff? That's Mr. Walt Slade — some folks call him *El Halcón* — Sheriff Calder's special deputy, who cleaned out the Palmer outfit, and Jason Helm, the bandit, and Waldron Lang and his bunch of killers. The owlhoots ain't got one bit of use for him. Wouldn't be surprised if it was him that hellion hoped to blow up."

"By gosh, I wouldn't be surprised if you're right," said he other. "*El Halcón!* Whe-e-ew!"

As they pulled up in front of the office, the door opened to reveal Deputy Zack Webley.

"Figured you'd be along so I unlocked," he explained. "Okay, bring it in."

The stretcher bearers, who apparently were not in the least fazed by their grisly task, wrapped the remains in a couple of blankets the hotel desk clerk had given them and deposited the grim bundle on the floor.

"Much obliged, boys," said the sheriff. "If

you want to look things over by daylight, come around tomorrow. Right now Mr. Slade craves nourishment; been a long time since his breakfast, and I can stand a small helpin' and a coupla snorts of redeye myself.

"And 'fore eating, we'll pick up your saddle pouches at the hotel," he added to Slade. "You're spending the night at my place; they'll be raisin' heck around that blasted hotel till past daylight. Might as well try to sleep in a boiler factory."

"An idea, all right," Slade agreed. "Thanks for your hospitality, I aim to take advantage of it."

The hotel and its environs were still bumbling like an overturned beehive when they secured the pouches. Then they proceeded to Fats Boyer's big restaurant and saloon, the Blue Bell. Lanky, saturnine Boyer greeted Slade warmly and led the way to his favorite table, from which he had a good view of the windows and the swinging doors, and a good part of the room as reflected in the backbar mirror.

"Heard you were in town and saved it for you," Boyer said. "Now I'll tell the cook who's here and he'll rustle something special for *El Halcón*. Waiter! drinks, and keep 'em coming. Everything on the house." He hustled to the kitchen.

The old Mexican cook looked out the door, waved to the sheriff, bowed low to *El Halcón,* and ducked back out of sight.

When the dinner arrived, it was all Boyer had claimed for it, and both Slade and the sheriff did the cook's offering full justice. After which the sheriff ordered another snort, Slade supped a final cup of fragrant coffee, and they smoked in silence, full-fed and content.

"My old Mexican cook and his boy will provide you with everything you need in the morning," Calder said. "Sleep as long as you want to; no sense in getting up early. Then we'll have a nice long talk and try and figure what's what. Oh, there's plenty besides what I've already told you. Town's in a normal condition, with the usual amount of hell raising. Bandits ambling across the river from Mexico every now and then. Outlaws riding the brush. A real rash of widelooping all of a sudden. Quite a few folks been killed, rather more than usual. You'll find plenty to keep you busy, as Captain McNelty said you would when he got my letter squawking for help."

Slade chuckled as he thought of what else Captain Jim, the famed Commander of the Border Battalion of the Texas Rangers, had to say about sheriffs in general and Tom

Calder in particular. To repeat it would evoke some vivid profanity on the part of Calder, so he decided not to. However, Calder and Captain Jim were old *amigos* and it was just to show affection that they spoke sarcastically of each other.

"Yes, hell-raising a-plenty," Calder continued. "Three stores here in town burgled. Two rumholes held up and robbed. Owner of one shot through the arm; didn't kill him. Which was more than could be said for a farmer driving a produce wagon down from Los Indios. Wagon was packing a hefty passel of money nobody was supposed to know about. Somebody knew, all right. The farmer was found dead under the seat, the money poke gone. Cow stealing right and left. Oh, it's a smooth and salty bunch working the section. Worse than the Palmer and Helm outfits of devils, which, as you know, is saying plenty. Hello! See the feller who just came in? That's Mostyn Selby, the owner of one of the saloons that was held up and robbed, the Albemarle. Sorta fine-looking feller, don't you think?"

Slade did think so. Mostyn Selby was a big man, fully six feet tall with broad shoulders and a deep chest. There was a lean, sinewy look to him. His face was straight-featured, deeply bronzed, with a

14

prominent nose and a powerful-appearing jaw and chin. His eyes, set deep in his head, were, Slade believed, a very light blue. His bearing was assured almost to the extent of a swagger. Looked to be a hard man and very likely was.

"Yep, the hellions, four of them, who somehow managed to slip in right after closing time and got the drop on him, cleaned the place of close onto a week's take that he had neglected to bank. Understand he makes a trip to the bank every day, now. Sorts snappin' the catch on the stable door after the cayuse has vamoosed. Seems some folks have to learn the hard way."

"Don't recall seeing him before," Slade remarked.

"Showed up not long after you were here last time," Calder said. "Bought the Albemarle from John Butler, John wanting to move west because this low-lying salt air was bad for his wife's health. John is pretty well-heeled with *dinero* and let the Albemarle go at a sacrifice; was glad to sell at any price. Selby sorta spruced it up and 'pears to be making a go of it. Not a bad-looking rumhole now."

Slade remembered the Albemarle, which was pretty run-down, the furnishings shoddy.

"Was Selby in the saloon business before establishing here?" he asked.

"In Dallas, I gather," the sheriff replied. "Heard he was in the cattle business over in that section, too. Wouldn't be surprised if he changed over a few years back when the cow business wasn't so good, especially for little owners."

"Probably," Slade said. "He should do all right here, with the town definitely on the upgrade."

"So I figure," Calder agreed. Slade nodded and forgot about Mostyn Selby for the time being, although new residents in a section always interested *El Halcón.*

Yes, Selby was a fine-looking man, but the sheriff felt that compared to the man sitting across from him, Selby was quite ordinary.

Walt Slade was very tall, more than six feet, and the breadth of his shoulders and the depth of his chest, which slimmed down to a narrow waist, were in keeping with his splendid height.

His face was as arresting as his form. A rather wide mouth, grin-quirked at the corners, relieved somewhat the tinge of fierceness evinced by the prominent hawk nose above and the powerful jaw and chin beneath. His hair, surmounting a broad forehead, was thick and crisp, and as black as his horse Shadow's midnight coat.

The sternly handsome countenance was dominated by long, black-lashed eyes of very pale gray, the gray of the sea under a stormy sky. Cold, reckless eyes that nevertheless always seemed to have gay little devils of laughter dancing in their clear depths. Devils that, did occasion warrant, would leap to the front and be anything but laughing. Then those eyes became "the terrible eyes of *El Halcón*," before the bleak stare of which armed and plenty salty men had been known to quail and hurriedly back down without making a hostile move.

Slade wore with careless grace the homely, efficient garb of the rangeland — Levis, the bibless overalls favored by cowhands, soft blue shirt with vivid neckerchief looped at his sinewy throat, well scuffed half-boots of softly tanned leather, and the broad-brimmed "J.B.," the rainshed of the plains, as the cowboys called a hat.

Around his waist were double cartridge belts, from the carefully worked and oiled cut-out holsters from which protruded the plain black butts of heavy guns. And from the butts of those Colt forty-fives, his slender, muscular hands seemed never far away.

"The singingest man in the whole Southwest, with the fastest gunhand," they called him. Right on both counts!

"Guess that bundle of dynamite was meant for you, all right, not much doubt about it," the sheriff remarked contemplatively.

"Probably," Slade admitted. "Crude, but efficient, sometimes. Enter the room by way of the convenient tree branch, lash a gun to a bed post or something, with the muzzle trained on the bundle of dynamite. A string tied to the trigger, other end to the door knob, the door is opened, outward. Down comes the gun hammer as the string tightens on the trigger. Off goes the gun, the slug whacks the bundle of explosive, and whoever opened the door goes through the ceiling. I encountered something similar once before, but caught on in time. Ever since, I've made sure a door is wide open and I'm not in line with it before I enter. Oh well, that's the way things work out. I'm going to bed."

"A notion," agreed Calder, pushing back his empty glass. "It's been a long, hard day. We'll discuss things more fully after you've had some rest. Grab your pouches and let's go! And keep your eyes skinned, I sorta figure somebody hereabouts don't like you over-well."

It was quite likely so, but they made it to the sheriff's *casa* without incident, where Slade, after warmly greeting the old cook and his helper, tumbled into bed and was almost instantly asleep.

2

Around midmorning he awoke, feeling greatly refreshed and ready for anything. He bathed, shaved, donned a clean shirt and overalls and went downstairs to breakfast, which the cook had ready and waiting.

"The *patron* to his office went, but soon he will return," said the cook. "He said for *Capitán* to it easy take."

After enjoying an appetizing meal, Slade did as the sheriff advised, taking it easy in the sumptuous living room until the old peace officer put in an appearance, which he did shortly.

"And now what?" he asked, accepting the snort the cook poured for him.

"Now," Slade replied, "I think I'll amble across the Rio Grande to Amado Menendez's La Luz cantina, in Matamoros, for a gab with him, and with Estevan, the head of his 'young men,' as he calls them, who help him keep order in the place. Not much goes on along the river, or elsewhere, they don't learn about."

"And you might get a word in with Dolores Malone, Amado's pretty little niece who, as everybody knows, really runs the place now. Smart as she's cute," the sheriff remarked innocently.

"By gosh! You're right. I might get to speak with her," Slade conceded. The sheriff shook with laughter.

Dolores Malone was a rather small girl with brains under her mop of curly black hair. Her complexion was creamily tanned, her sweetly turned lips vividly red. Her astonishingly big eyes were darkly blue, the blue of wisteria in the rain. Her small figure certainly left nothing to be desired.

Her father had been a handsome, rollicking Irish soldier of fortune who had married Amado Menendez's oldest sister who, like Dolores, had inherited the famed beauty of the Menendez women. The older sister had died shortly before her Irish husband passed on, leaving Dolores an orphan. Amado would have gladly supported Dolores, as he had his younger sister, who was but a few years older than her attractive niece, before she married Tol Grundy, a cantina owner. But Dolores held that a Texas girl capable of supporting

21

herself should not be dependent on others. So she started dancing in Amado's cantina and helping him in various ways, gradually rising to her present position as the real driving force behind La Luz, the cantina.

Yes, Walt Slade knew Dolores Malone very well indeed, and greatly admired the roses that grew so profusely around Dolores' little house on Jackson Street. Which was the reason for Sheriff Calder's laughter.

"Going to ride?" he asked.

Slade shook his head. "It's a nice day and it isn't far, so I think I'll walk," he decided.

"Okay," said Calder. "Meet me at the Blue Bell for dinner?"

"Yes, I'll do that," Slade promised.

"Okay," the sheriff repeated. "Doc Cooper figures to hold an inquest on what's left of the dynamiter. You don't have to attend unless you feel like it. I'll have to be present to lend official dignity to the occasion. Won't do to only have the coroner and the work dodgers he calls a jury present."

"Chances are I'll attend, just for the novelty of the thing."

"Novelty!" snorted Calder. "Oh, I get it, the novelty being the killing of a horned toad you didn't have a hand in. Betcha the next one won't be a 'novelty.' "

Slade laughed and strolled out. He sauntered slowly toward the approach to the Gateway Bridge at the foot of Fourteenth Street, S.E., replying to greetings called by folks who remembered him from previous visits. Finally, after several pauses, he drew near the beginning of the approach. At a hitch rack nearby stood two horses, and there were people about the foot of the ramp. And right where the upward slant began, two individuals, apparently repair men, were busy at work on the bridge railing. Slade glanced at them, and abruptly noted something that heightened his interest in the apparently innocuous pair.

Interested him so much so that instantly every sense was at hairtrigger alertness.

So when the pair whirled to face him, hands streaking to holsters, *El Halcón* was ready, going sideways and down and whipping out both Colts even as a gun blazed and the slug fanned his face. Prone on the bridge floor he shot with both hands, again and yet again.

One of the "workmen" plunged down on his face. Answering bullets hammered the side sheet under the railing, hissing over the prostrate Ranger. The second gunslinger leaped forward, halted as if struck by a pile driver, whirled around, and fell. He waited for a moment, then stiffened and lay motionless beside his dead companion. A glance told Slade they were both satisfactorily cared for. He stood up, ejecting the spent shells from his Colts and replacing them with fresh cartridges.

The group at the foot of the ramp had scattered in every direction when lead started flying and were now yelling and cursing.

"I saw it all!" a man shouted. "The devils tried to kill Mr. Slade, but he was too fast for the blankety-blank-blanks! Good work, Mr. Slade, almighty good work.

"How'd you catch on so fast, Mr. Slade?" he asked as the chattering crowd converged on *El Halcón.*

"I just happened to notice something that aroused my interest in them," Slade explained. "One of the men was wielding a tool very awkwardly — with his *left* hand, apparently anxious to keep his *right* free. I wondered why, and when his right hand slid to his holster, I had a pretty good notion as to just what he *did* have in mind. Would appear I guessed right."

There was a moment of astonished silence, then a chorus of admiring exclamations.

"Would 'pear the Mexican boys have the right of it when they say, 'The eye of *El Hal-*

cón sees all'!" chuckled one oldtimer, shaking his grizzled head. Before the others could get started, Slade deftly changed the topic of conversation.

"Will somebody kindly run up to the sheriff's office and fetch him," he requested. "I want him to view the situation as is. If he's not in his office, you may find him at the Blue Bell."

Several individuals hurried off to take care of the chore.

Down the ramp, from Matamoros, came a tall young man with snapping black eyes and a dark, savage face, who seemed to glide rather than walk. It was Estevan, the Mexican-Yaqui knife man. He and Slade were old *amigos* and had a hearty greeting for each other.

"Capitán," said Estevan, conferring the Mexican term of respect, "told were we you were in town, and when the shooting I heard, knew I that *Capitán* was at work. So hurried I on the chance that my thirsty blade might something of help to *Capitán* be.

"But," he added regretfully, "late am I and the fun missed I."

"*Gracias* for your good intentions," Slade replied smilingly. "Now if you don't mind, hustle back to Amado's cantina and tell him and Dolores everything is under control and that I'll be with them shortly. Right now I'm waiting for the sheriff."

"Of a certainty, *Capitán*," the knife man answered and sped back up the ramp.

Sheriff Calder arrived before long, glanced at the two motionless forms.

"After you hot and heavy, eh?" he remarked. "How'd they try to work it?"

Slade told him. He shook his head resignedly. "Is there ever anything you don't see?" he sighed.

"It was quite obvious," Slade replied. "One of the little slips the owlhoot brand always seems prone to make. Awkwardly trying to manipulate a tool backward made me wonder just a little. So naturally I became interested in them, and when they made their move I was ready for them. Nothing to it."

"Oh, sure!" Calder snorted sarcastically. "Have you looked them over?"

"I preferred for you to see them as they are," Slade said. "We'll examine them fully after we get them to the office."

"A good notion," the sheriff agreed. "Here come Gus and Webley, my work-dodging deputies; they'll take over. Lend them a hand, some of you fellers," he requested the crowd, which was pressing close, constantly augmented by fresh arrivals.

A couple of shutters were detached from a nearby building and the grim procession got under way, collecting adherents until the office was crowded when the bodies were laid out on the floor for inspection.

Immediately heated arguments developed as to whether the two drygulchers had ever been seen in town; if so, where, under what conditions, in whose company. There was such a difference of opinion that Slade felt the various assertions were of little value.

The remains of the dynamiter of the night before were uncovered, with the arguments going full swing again. Finally Calder cleared the office and locked the door. He and Slade agreed with the disputants to the effect that all three were unsavory-looking specimens. Slade examined the hands of all three, including the dynamiter's detached one.

"Have been cowhands, but quite a while back," he deduced. "Hands of all three show faint marks of rope and branding iron. One thing is sure, the pair who made the try for me on the bridge were certainly never mechanics. The result: the kind of a little slip the owlhoot brand always makes sooner or later, in one way or another. So far as those two were concerned, the slip, small though it was, proved fatal."

"Uh-huh, with an *El Halcón* to notice the slip," the sheriff commented dryly. "Say! quite a bit of *dinero* in the pockets, more than the horned toads ever got from honest work."

"Well, you gave me to understand that the bunch has been doing right well by itself."

"Too blankety-blank-blank well," growled Calder. "Anything else in this junk their pockets coughed up that interests you?" Slade shook his head.

"Well, Doc Cooper can hold an inquest on all three tonight," the sheriff continued. "Now what you got in mind?"

"Now I'm going to make another try for Matamoros and Amado's cantina," Slade replied. "See you at the Blue Bell around dark."

Slade received even more greetings than formerly as he made his way to the bridge, but he finally managed to get across to Matamoros without further mishap. He passed slowly through the City Market, typically Mexican, vibrant with colors and filled with odors and sounds, which always interested the Ranger, and reached the softly lighted, tastefully furnished cantina.

Estevan was at the end of the bar when he entered, while Amado and Dolores Malone

28

were busy at a table decorated with flowers, bottles of golden wine, silver and crystal. Dolores came dancing across to greet him, both little sun-golden hands outstretched. He cupped his hands around her slender waist, tossed her into the air and caught her, squealing and laughing, as she came down. She clung to him, her big eyes sparkling, her little white teeth flashing against the vivid red of her lips.

"Oh, it's so good to see you again!" she chattered. "And so much sooner than I expected. How neglected all the beautiful ladies you passed on the way must feel!"

"Why, I didn't notice any," he replied, his expression all innocence. Dolores didn't appear impressed.

"Never mind," she said with a giggle. "Now my roses won't be lonesome."

"The party will we have," Amado said as they shook hands. "The *Señor* Sheriff must here be also. Him we will send for at once. And your old *amigo*, the *jefe politico* — the Chief of Police — will here be also. Be seated, *Capitán,* and of the golden wine partake."

Slade complied. Dolores perched beside him.

The sheriff rolled in, to the accompaniment of an hilarious welcome. Soon after-

29

ward, the old Matamoros police chief arrived with an effusive greeting for Slade.

"Most welcome you are, *Capitán*," he said. "Now indeed will soon all be well."

"Hope I don't disappoint you," Slade returned.

"You won't," the chief stated positively.

It was inevitable that for a while the conversation dealt with the attempt on Slade's life. Amado applauded the downing of the two killers as did the chief. Dolores sighed, and her beautiful eyes were worried.

"I suppose I should be used to it by now," she said. "But I just can't keep from getting the jitters."

"Remember what he says, that if your number ain't up on the board, nobody can put it up," the sheriff reminded.

"A comforting philosophy, at least," Dolores conceded. "Darn it, I'm hungry!"

"That will be taken care of the very soon," said Amado. "The cook his orders has."

The sun set in polychromatic glory, the dark closed down. With the advent of night, La Luz was filling up, and the party was going strong. It was gay, colorful, and Slade enjoyed it but not wholeheartedly, for his thoughts were largely elsewhere. He hadn't been sent into the section to be the center of attraction in a welcoming celebration, but to ferret out and bring to justice certain miscreants. And so far he appeared to be getting exactly nowhere with the task.

However, he was forced to admit that perhaps he was being just a little bit impatient; he had been in the section less than twenty-four hours, scant time to get anything like a line-up on conditions. And, everything taken into consideration, he hadn't done too bad. Killing the two outlaws who attempted his life helped some, and he was indirectly responsible for the death of the dynamiter. A start, anyhow.

But the disturbing fact was that if an organized outfit was operating in the section, and he believed that to be the case, them was no doubt but that some fresh atrocity was being planned, in the course of which some innocent person might well die. It was up to him to try and anticipate what the devils had in mind and take steps to thwart it. And he had not the slightest idea who they were.

Oh, well! Perhaps things would work out; always seemed to. He shrugged his broad shoulders and dismissed the problem for the time being. Might as well enjoy himself when he had the chance. "Lovely Thaïs sits beside thee. Take the goods the gods provide thee."

And he seriously doubted that Alexander's Thaïs was more lovely and charming than she who *did* sit beside him, her adoring eyes following his every move.

The sheriff chuckled. "Guess Doc will have to get along with the deputies supervising his inquest," he remarked. "Well, the hotel clerk is the only one with any notion as to how the dynamiter got his come-uppance, and a dozen men will swear Walt shot in self-defense, in the performance of his duty as a law enforcement officer, so he'll make out."

Slade nodded agreement; border country inquests were informal affairs, with the jury's verdict usually a foregone conclusion. Yes, Doc would make out.

"Business is sure picking up," remarked Dolores. "I think I'd better get out onto the floor for a while — not enough girls to go around. Be seeing you, dear. Try and keep out of trouble while I do a few numbers." She bounded off to the dance floor.

Amado was needed at the far end of the bar. Estevan decided to scout around a bit outside. The police chief recalled an unfinished chore and also departed for awhile. Slade and the sheriff were left alone at the table.

3

Due to his habit of working alone whenever possible and not revealing his Ranger connections, Walt Slade had built up a peculiar dual reputation. Those who knew the truth maintained he was not only the most fearless but the ablest of the Rangers as well. But others, who knew him only as *El Halcón,* with killings to his credit and a habit of horning in on good things others had started, vigorously declared he was just an owlhoot himself, too smart to get caught so far, but who'd slip up sooner or later and get his deserved comeuppance.

Others of this group, however, were his stanch defenders, pointing out that he always worked on the side of law and order, often with peace officers of impeccable reputation, like Tom Calder, for instance, and anybody he killed had a killing overdue.

The deception worried Captain McNelty, who feared his lieutenant and ace undercover man might come to harm because of it. But Slade pointed out that as *El Halcón* of dubious reputation in some quarters, avenues of information were opened to him that would be closed to a known Ranger, and that outlaws, thinking him very likely one of their own brand, sometimes grew careless, to their grief.

So Captain Jim did not definitely forbid the deception, and Slade went his carefree way as *El Halcón,* satisfied with what the past had brought forth, and with the present, and bothering about the future none at all. And treasuring most what was said by the *peónes* and other humble folk.

"*El Halcón!* The good, the just, the compassionate, the friend of the lowly of all who know sorrow or trouble or persecution. May *El Dios* ever guard him!"

The sheriff ordered another snort, Slade more coffee. They relaxed in comfortable silence, each busy with his own thoughts.

From the harbor a whistle wailed. Almost instantly it was joined by others, a regular witches' carnival of eldritch shrieks and screams.

"What in blazes?" barked the sheriff.

"Must be a fire," Slade said. "Let's go see."

They hurried out. A red glare was mounting the slant of the northern sky. As they headed for the bridge, Estevan glided in beside them.

"The river across," he said. Slade nodded and quickened the pace.

Another moment and they saw it. A building on the north waterfront was a seething mass of flames.

"It's the big Cascade Company warehouse!" exclaimed Calder. "Now how in blazes did that catch, I wonder?"

As they sped up the ramp, a drumming of fast hoofs sounded on the crown of the bridge. Into view barged four horsemen, hatbrims drawn low, neckerchiefs up high, until of their faces was to be seen little more than a glint of eyes. They gave startled yelps as they spotted *El Halcón* and his companions.

"Look out! Duck!" Slade roared as he saw hands streak to holsters. He was going sideways along the bridge rails as the guns blazed and slugs whizzed past, close. Both his Colts let go with a rattling crash.

A rider spun from the saddle to thud on the floor boards. Slade shot again as a bullet barely touched his temple, hurling him nearly off balance with the shock, but a second saddle was emptied. The sheriff's forty-five boomed and still another of the attackers was accounted for. The hiss of Estevan's throwing blade was echoed by a bubbling scream, and there were four riderless horses careening down the ramp, snorting their fright.

"All four accounted for," the sheriff added an instant later. "A quick look and then on across the bridge. The Matamoros Police Chief will take care of things here and have an explanation that will absolve us. Which will be all to the good; we can do without international entanglements." He barely glanced at the dead men, knowing the chief would arrange for him to examine them later. Estevan retrieved his knife from a dead throat, wiped it on a shirt, and they headed for the north shore at a fast pace.

"Imagine — everybody is so interested in the fire that they didn't pay any mind to the shooting, probably thinking it was just somebody sounding the alarm, a common practice," Slade remarked.

"Wonder why those devils threw down on us like they did?" said Calder.

"I think," Slade replied, "that you'll find that they had something to do with the fire. Also, I'm of the opinion that we did for four more of that owlhoot outfit working the section. Which helps."

"You're darn right," agreed Calder. "Reckon the devils are beginning to understand just what it does mean to be bucking *El Halcón*."

"They were caught off balance," Slade said. "I imagine we were the last persons in the world they expected to meet."

"Well, we *were* the last persons in this world they met," the sheriff pointed out, with grim humor. "Here comes the fire department — listen to the bells! But I'm scairt that warehouse is a goner. If those devils did set the fire, I wonder why?"

"Must have been some reason for so doing," Slade replied. "Perhaps we'll soon find out. By the way, is there a night watchman on duty there, do you know?"

"By gosh, come to think of it there is, or supposed to be," the sheriff replied. Slade nodded, and quickened the pace. A few more minutes and they were mingling with the crowd milling about the burning building.

"There's one of the warehouse clerks," Calder said. "Hey, Chet," he called, "where's the night watchman?"

"Sheriff, I don't know," the clerk answered. "He sure ain't one of the bunch out here. Do you think — ?"

"Listen," Slade interrupted, "there's a

back door to the shack, is there not? Yes? Lead us to it, fast."

The clerk obeyed and a few moments later they were at the back of the building, which the fire hadn't yet reached, with the door before them. The clerk ran to it, tried the knob. "Locked!" he announced.

"Stand away," Slade told him and launched his two hundred pounds of bone and muscle against the door.

There was a screech of ruptured metal, a splintering of wood, and the door banged open. Blistering hot air gushed out, and a cloud of smoke.

"Watchman may have made it to the back, if he wasn't killed," Slade said. "Stay here, all of you, and keep watch." With which he dived into the smoke-filled room.

He gasped as the full force of the heat struck him squarely, gulped a smoky breath, ducked his head and forged forward. As he had figured there would be, there was a narrow aisle between stacks of merchandise. Gasping and choking, he dropped to hands and knees, holding his head as low as possible, catching a faint current of air flowing along the floor. The building was very long, front to rear, and it seemed that an enormous distance stretched ahead of him.

Grimly, he crept on. Little flickers of light

filtered through the smoky gloom. He strained his eyes for a glimpse of what he expected to see, for his hunch indicated it was somewhere in the narrow aisle. The heat was like the breath of a blast furnace, the smoke thickening. Then, peering ahead, he saw his hunch was a straight one. Sprawled on the floor was the motionless form of a man. Yes, the hunch was a straight one. The watchman, doubtless injured, had tried to make it to the back door and been overcome by the heat and smoke.

Reaching the still body, Slade felt of the man's heart. It was beating, feebly; there was not a moment to lose. He gripped the bulky form and surged erect. Reeling, staggering, he lurched back toward the door. His head was one vast agony, his lungs bursting. Red flashes blazed before his eyes, bell notes stormed in his ears. His whirling senses were leaving him. Overhead was a creaking and groaning; any minute and the roof would fall in. Which would mean the finish for both of them. Yes, it looked like curtains!

Then abruptly he realized he was breathing clear air, and that hands were gripping him, the heavy burden plucked from his sagging arms. From a great distance, Sheriff Calder's voice reached him —

"Easy! Take it easy! You're out! We've got him. Easy now, and catch your breath."

Dimly he realized Estevan's strong arms were around him, supporting him, and that Estevan was swearing in three languages.

Quickly his brain cleared, his strength came surging back and he was able to stand without support. Now he heard the sheriff's voice very clearly as he roared for someone to bring the doctor. Men were carrying the limp form of the unconscious watchman farther away from the fire.

"Just in time!" whooped Calder. "There goes the roof!"

With a terrific crash the roof fell in, and the whole building became a shapeless mass, spouting flame and smoke in every direction, forcing them to move still farther away.

The watchman was placed on a blanket. Slade knelt beside him, pleased to note his heartbeat was stronger. He had an ugly gash in the side of his head, just above the back of the left temple, but Slade's sensitive fingers could ascertain no indication of fracture.

"Should make it," was his verdict. "Got a mean wallop with a gun barrel, I'd say, and swallowed a lot of smoke, but he'll make it. Should be regaining consciousness before long."

"And then maybe he can tell us what happened and what's the meaning of all this," added Calder.

"I've a notion I can tell you what's the meaning of it, Sheriff," said a voice behind them.

The sheriff turned to face the speaker, an elderly, portly individual.

"Why, hello, Chris!" he said. "Walt, this is Chris Preston, the warehouse manager. What you figure it's all about, Chris?"

"That there was a tidy sum of money in the office safe," Preston replied. "Reckon that was what the devils were after. It was payment in cash for a big order of goods by a Mexican outfit. You know the Mexicans prefer to deal in cash, and it was too late to make the bank. I thought nobody but me and the Mexican purchaser knew about it. Guess I was wrong." Slade thought he was probably right in his guess.

"Here comes Doc Cooper," somebody on the outskirts of the crowd shouted.

The old Frontier practitioner hove into view, glanced at the watchman, nodded to Slade.

"Any indications of fracture?" he asked.

"None that I could ascertain," *El Halcón* replied.

41

"Then there ain't any," grunted the doctor. "Those fingers of yours are never wrong. Okay, I'll give him a stimulant and patch him up. That should bring him out of it. Pulse is okay. So is his breathing."

With which he opened his satchel and got busy. Slade rolled a cigarette and watched the operation.

Cooper was right. In a very few mintues after he completed his ministrations, the watchman opened his eyes and stared blankly. He muttered something, blinked his eyes and, with the help of Slade and the doctor, sat up.

"Send somebody for some hot coffee," Slade told the manager. He rolled a cigarette and gave it to the watchman, who nodded gratefully and puffed hard, his eyes clearing.

After glancing inquiringly at the doctor, who nodded, the manager said,

"Think you can tell us what happened, Orn?"

"Reckon there ain't much to tell," mumbled the watchman. "I was puttin' my lunch on the office table when I heard something behind me. I looked around and saw five hellions with black rags tied over their faces, and guns in their hands. I started to stand up, but one of them, a big tall, broad-shouldered devil, clouted me with a gun barrel and knocked me to the floor. I was sorta dazed, but had sense enough not to move. Figured if I did, he'd finish me off. They began boring holes in the safe door. In a little bit, they pulled the combination knob out and opened the door. Took the money out and stuck it in a bag the big one carried. Just as they started toward the outside door, there was talking somewhere on the street. The big one took a swipe at the lamp on the table, the only one lighted. Knocked it off the table. The bowl broke and spattered oil in every direction, but the wick didn't go out and things began to burn. The devils hustled out the door and banged it shut. I tried to stand up, but my head came near bustin' and I reckon I really did pass out for a while. When I come to, it was almighty hot, there was fire all around me and the place was full of smoke. I came nigh to choking but I managed to crawl to the door leading in back and pulled it shut after me. Then I reckon after I'd crawled a little more through the smoke the place was full of, I passed out again. That's all I remember. How'd I get out?"

"Mr. Slade packed you out, and came nigh to getting his own comeuppance doing it," the manager told him. He shot the

Ranger a grateful glance, but before he could put his feelings in words, Slade interrupted with,

"You say there were five of the robbers?"

"That's right," the watchman said. "I'm sure of it."

"Hmmm!" interpolated the sheriff, "thought there were only four."

"There were five," the watchman repeated. Slade and the sheriff exchanged understanding glances.

"I'm sorry I wasn't able to do a better job, Mr. Preston," the watchman said.

"Never you mind about that," replied the manager, patting his shoulder. "The money and building loss don't mean too much; we're insured. I'm only thankful nothing really bad happened to you. Here's your coffee. Get on the outside of it, be good for you."

Old Orn proceeded to do so. The sheriff speculated over the smoking ruins the fire fighters had drenched to little more than a smolder.

"Well," he said, "don't see as there's anything else we can do here, so we might as well get back to our party; be seeing you, everybody."

"And thanks again, Mr. Slade, for saving this old coot from getting roasted," said the manager, bestowing another pat on the old fellow's shoulder.

"And I'm sure plumb beholden to you, Mr. Slade," Orn added. "Hope the time will come when maybe I can sorta return the favor."

As they moved up the ramp on the way to Matamoros, Calder repeated what Orn had said — "Five of the devils; and what in blazes does that mean? We only did for four."

"It means," Slade replied, "that the head of the pack made it in the clear, with the money. He didn't cross the bridge. Sent his followers along as a decoy, with folks perhaps chasing them along the Camino Real from Matamoros, while he was snugged in town somewhere with the *dinero.* Very, very clever! And if we hadn't happened along just when we did, they would have gotten away with it. And as for him, he did all right by himself, making a very nice haul."

"The blankety-blank-blank!" growled Calder. "Well, his time will come. Wonder who in blazes he is?"

"It is imperative that we find out," Slade answered. "I've a notion, Tom, that we'll find we are up against one of the very smoothest characters we have ever contacted, which is saying plenty."

"He ain't going to be smooth enough, now he has *El Halcón* to deal with," the sheriff declared. "Just a matter of time. By the way, Doc Cooper said the inquest came off okay, with the usual verdict. Gus and Webley, the deputies, were there, of course. Doc said they came out to look at the fire but decided they'd better stick around the office in case I'd want them. I asked him to tell them everything was under control; to shut up shop for the night. Yep, where that horned toad who slid out of the loop is concerned, just a matter of time."

"Hope you're right," Slade said, smiling. "Well, here we are at the cantina, and appears everybody is outside."

"And your little gal with the jitters, I'll bet on that," chuckled Calder. "Here she comes, on the run!"

Dolores was indeed snuggled in Slade's arms, trying hard to smile through the tears that gemmed her long lashes.

"I couldn't keep from worrying," she said. "Even though the police chief did assure us you must be all right, seeing there were four dead men on the bridge and you weren't around, that you must have come out on top in the gun battle. That's what he told us privately. Said to everybody else that evidently those fellows had a falling out over

46

something and killed one another."

"The chief's all right," said Calder. "That's the report he'll make to the commandant of the *rurales,* the Mexican mounted police, and it will be accepted without question. Does away with the chance of entanglements because of us operating on this side of the river. Walt could get by, seeing as he holds a commission in the *rurales* from the Governor of the State of Chihuahua, but they might look sorta sideways at Estevan and me. Yep, the chief is all right."

Amado turned to the door. "In come," said he. "The party will again begin."

"Fine!" applauded the sheriff. "I'm plumb starved."

"Me, too," Dolores agreed. Slade and Estevan also intimated they could stand a bite.

The police chief sauntered in, accepted a chair and a glass of wine.

"*Ai!* It is a wicked world," he sighed, glancing expectantly at Slade, who obliged with an account of what happened on the bridge. The chief nodded approval.

"The world those four will not miss," he said.

Slade also detailed the robbery and the burning of the warehouse for the chief's benefit. The sheriff presented his own ver-

47

sion of Slade's rescue of old Orn, the night watchman.

"Not that there was anything unusual about it," he concluded. "He's all the time doing things like that."

"*Si,*" agreed the chief. "Verily, as was said of Our Lord in the days of old, he goes about doing good!"

4

Amado, declining something to eat, took up his post at the far end of the bar. Estevan slipped out to scout around a bit.

"Hello!" exclaimed the sheriff, "here comes Mostyn Selby, the owner of the Albemarle, you know, which was held up. Remember, I pointed him out in the Blue Bell."

Selby waved to the sheriff, glanced at Slade, and joined Amado, whom he began talking with.

"He'd like to open a place on this side of the river," Dolores said. "He's been discussing it with Uncle Amado. Says the town is going to be up and coming."

"He's right," Slade agreed. "Already quite a bit of tourist trade is showing up here, and more will be attracted to Matamoros."

"Oh, I'd say he's a smart operator, even though he did get careless and keep too much money in his saloon," remarked

Calder. "Guess everybody makes a mistake, now and then, Walt excepted."

"Hope he agrees with you," Dolores said cheerfully.

The police chief emptied his glass, glanced at the clock.

"Would *Capitán* like the bodies of those four *ladrones* to view?" he suggested. "In my office, laid out for him who undertakes, they are."

"A good idea," Slade replied. "Let's go."

"And try not to get mixed up in anything more," Dolores begged. "While you're gone, I'll change to a street dress and be ready to traipse across the bridge with you. That bite to eat revived my strength."

"You'll need it," the sheriff predicted with a grin. Dolores pointedly ignored him.

Arriving at the chief's office, they scanned the four hardlined faces with nothing outstanding about any of them, in Slade's opinion. He carefully examined the dead hands.

"Two of them were cowhands quite a while back, marks of rope and a branding iron show that. The other two, no."

"What the devil are they?" wondered the sheriff. Slade shrugged.

"Well, there's no lack of river and Gulf pirates and similar gentry hereabouts, who

50

are ready for anything that provides them with spending money."

"Quite a bit of money in their pockets was," observed the chief.

"We'll pay for burying then," Slade said. "And the horses they rode, good animals, should bring quite a bit more, if you manage to round them up."

"Round them up we will," promised the chief. "On the table is all else their pockets gave forth."

Slade glanced at the scattering of odds and ends range riders usually carry, but discovered nothing he considered of interest.

"Well, guess there's nothing more we can do here," he said. "Thanks, *amigo,* for everything," he told the chief. "Always you are a big help."

"To help *El Halcón,* the good, the just, the compassionate, is always the honor great," the chief replied, and bowed.

As they headed for the cantina, Calder remarked, "Well, we did a pretty good chore of combining pleasure and business. A life saved and four rapscallions done for. Not bad at all."

"Not bad," Slade agreed. "Could have been better, though, if the kingpin of the lot hadn't slid out of the loop."

"His time will come," was the sheriff's confident rejoinder.

When they reached the cantina, the crowd had pretty well thinned out. Amado had sounded his last call. Dolores had changed, and after saying goodnight to everybody, including the cook and the kitchen help, they departed.

As they crossed the bridge, Dolores snuggled close and whispered,

"What are you thinking about, dear?"

"Roses!"

Late the next afternoon, Slade and Calder sat in the sheriff's office and discussed the situation as it stood, with no very satisfying conclusions. That there was a mastermind somewhere who planned and supervised the raids, both were convinced. But who it was they had not the slightest idea. Finally the sheriff gave vent to a disgusted rumble.

"Oh, heck!" he said, "let's amble over to the Blue Bell for a snort and a snack. Everybody shows up in the Blue Bell sooner or later; maybe we'll spot something."

Slade was agreeable and after locking the door, they made their way to the saloon and occupied the table Boyer always had reserved for them.

"Hello! there's another jigger who squatted here since you were last in the diggin's," Calder said. "The feller talking with Boyer. Name's Sefton, Vibart Sefton."

Slade regarded Sefton with interest. He was a big, rough-looking man, powerfully built, and tall. His features were craggy, with a very prominent nose, small, deep-set eyes, a great square jowl and a heavy chin. His forehead was massive, and his pushed-back black "J.B." disclosed thick dark hair slightly sprinkled with gray. The afternoon was warm and he had discarded his coat, revealing arms bulging with muscle. Slade noted that the upper half of one ear was unduly thick and swollen. He judged his age to be between thirty-five and forty, probably nearer forty. Anyhow, in the prime of life.

"What would you say his business is?" the sheriff asked.

"Well," Slade smiled, "from that cauliflower ear and those arms, I'd say he is or has been either a prize fighter or a wrestler."

"Wrong on both counts," chuckled Calder. "He's a land speculator and a lawyer, a darn good one."

"The last thing I would have guessed," Slade said. "Although that forehead, I'd say, denotes far above average in intelligence. As for the rest of him, it just goes to show you can't judge by appearances."

"But just the same he's a tough hombre," replied the sheriff. "Sorta unhealthy to take liberties with him. A coupla supposed-to-be salty jiggers he was mixed up with in one of his land deals tried to bring trouble to him. He cleaned 'em both quicker than you could say scat."

Slade nodded, not at all surprised. "You say he has been doing all right with his land speculating and law practice?" he remarked.

"That's so," said Calder. "Yep, he's been doing all right. You know what conditions were quite some years back. Sorta cooled down after the Cortinas invasion and the war, but recently it has steadily revived."

Slade knew of an unsavory practice of favoritism on the part of various unscrupulous Texas politicians that resulted, in some instances, in the loss of property among Mexican landholders north of the Rio Grande. It didn't make for good feeling south of the river. Nor had Texas owners been altogether immune. Now it appeared a close-knit, skillfully organized combine was at work and extending its powers.

Walt Slade viewed this with decided disfavor. Organized outlaws were bad enough, but a Border war was infinitely worse. It could drench the section with blood, something he earnestly hoped to prevent, and which, as a Texas Ranger, it was his duty to prevent if humanly possible.

And such an individual as Vibart Sefton might well provide the spark that would, perhaps unwittingly, start the conflagration. For he gathered from what the sheriff said of him that Sefton was bucking the combine, going it alone, for his own purposes. And the combine would not take kindly to that.

The combine, Slade believed, was similar to, though not operating so openly as, the notorious Land Committee at Laredo he had managed to bring to justice before.

"Well," he mused to himself, "time that grinds the rocks will tell us all." With which he dismissed Vibart Sefton and the combine from his thoughts, for the time being, and proceeded to enjoy his coffee and snack.

However, after they had finished eating, the conversation, not unnaturally, turned back to Vibart Sefton, who was still talking with Fats Boyer.

"You said, I believe, that Sefton has been doing very well as a lawyer," Slade remarked. "Just how?"

"Well," replied the sheriff, "somebody, nobody seems to know just who started it, but claims were put against the land held by some Mexican-Texans, lands secured by grants from the Spanish King when all this section was a part of New Spain, as they called it. The fellers couldn't produce their grants. They'd been lost, misplaced, stolen, or something. So Sefton got busy for those fellers. He dug up old papers, diaries, transactions in which the grants were mentioned, years and years ago, deals, land transfers and such. Mentioned as a matter of course in connection with such matters. The result was, the courts held that the grants had undoubtedly been issued and that the holdings mentioned were valid. The jiggers hung onto their holdings." The sheriff paused to light his pipe, and when it was going to his satisfaction, he resumed:

"When somebody mentioned to him that he'd sure done some folks a good turn, his answer was what I figure was typical for him."

"What was his answer?" Slade asked. The sheriff chuckled.

"He said, 'Hell! I don't calc'late to do people a good turn. I'm out to make money. A lawyer has to eat same as anybody else.' "

Slade smiled, and his interest in Vibart Sefton mounted.

"And he showed several store owners and rumhole keepers how to get a better deal on the money they'd borrowed," Calder continued. "And things like that. Oh, he's a smart one, all right. Wouldn't be surprised that, sooner or later, a lot of folks are going to be flabbergasted to learn how smart, in a lot of ways, he really is."

"Now what do you mean by that?" Slade asked.

"Oh, nothing, just thinking," the sheriff evaded.

"Well, don't do too much thinking out loud," Slade advised. "You might be doing somebody an injustice." Calder shrugged, and did not pursue the topic. Slade ordered more coffee and thoughtfully studied Vibart Sefton. He knew that Calder was suspicious of Sefton and his motives, and when old Tim got a notion firmly implanted in his grizzled noggin, he was very hard to change.

"Figure to amble over to Matamoros and Amado's cantina later?" the sheriff asked.

"Unless something happens to alter my intention," Slade said.

"Something is liable to happen any minute in this blasted loco pueblo," Calder growled. "A feller could risk holding his breath till something busts loose; he wouldn't choke."

"Would appear you are in a pessimistic mood this afternoon," Slade smiled. The sheriff grunted and didn't argue the point,

57

compromising on ordering another snort of redeye.

"By the way," he remarked, "do you figure those hellions deliberately set fire to the warehouse last night, maybe to cover up the safe robbery?"

"Frankly, I don't," Slade answered. "I would say that was the unexpected result of some fast thinking on the part of the head of the outfit. When he heard voices approaching, as the watchman mentioned, he had no way of knowing who or what they were and knew that in the lighted office he would be at a disadvantage. I figure he intended to strike the burner of the lamp and extinguish it. But he slipped a little and struck a trifle low, braking the bowl and sending oil flying in every direction. The still-burning wick took care of that, and up went the warehouse. Oh, he's a shrewd one, all right, but human, I suppose, like the rest of us, and therefore not infallible.

"Just the same however, I fear he is going to take considerable running down."

The sheriff indulged in one of his favorite remarks, "Just a matter of time."

"But very likely some lively times for us in the interim," Slade predicted. "Right now our foremost problem, aside from establishing his identity, is to anticipate where he will strike next. Got any notions?" The sheriff did a little more repeating.

"So darn many things the hellions can hit," he complained. "Trains, stage coaches, banks, stores, rumholes, and the devil only knows what else."

"Right," Slade conceded. "So, as we have done before, let's do a little checking on things an outlaw bunch might find attractive. Suppose we start here and work west for a ways. First is Santa Rita, a few miles west of Brownsville, which was the ranch home and headquarters of Cheno Cartinas, called the Red Robber of the Rio Grande, who many years ago actually invaded Brownsville and held the American town of several thousand captive for forty-eight hours, looting and slaying. Nothing much left of Santa Rita, however, just a few old adobe shacks that look to have been there since the Flood. No dice where Santa Rita is concerned. Next we come to La Paloma, prettily named for a song, but not particularly melodious at present. Write off La Paloma. The next town, so called, Los Indios — that started out as a ranch. Several big ones in the vicinity now."

"And they all say they've been losing stock," the sheriff put in. "Incidentally, as you'll remember, there's a stage line from

Los Indios to here. Comes down from Pharr, up to the north, and turns east on the river trail."

"Something to give thought to," Slade said. "Also the widelooping angle — that might provide us with opportunity, it has done so before. Santa Maria, seven or eight miles west of Los Indios, we can keep in mind, there being pump irrigation and rich farmlands in the vicinity. Progresso next, mighty little progressive about it. We can pass it by.

"Now, as you know, the trail bears close to the windings of the Rio Grande and a couple of miles or so over to the river is Hidalgo, which is really of interest and will bear watching. On the south side of the river is the Mexican town of Reynosa, and there is no doubt but that extensive smuggling goes on there, meaning a lot of money changing hands. Which very likely our outlaw bunch knows as well as we do and might well seek to turn the knowledge to their advantage, and which might also provide us with a mite of opportunity. Hidalgo we'll keep very much in mind.

"So we've covered about thirty miles to the west, which should do in that direction for the present. Now what have you to suggest?"

"Well, for one thing there's the railroad from here to Port Isabel. And the stage line that comes down from Alice, and the one from Pharr. They sometimes pack quite a hefty sum of *dinero*. And I'd say the wide-looping that has been going strong the past few months is something to think about."

"Definitely," Slade agreed. "So all in all, we have plenty of ground to cover. Ought to be able to root something out, with all that territory to cover. We've just got to be at the right place at the right time."

"Uh-huh, that's all," the sheriff conceded wearily. "There goes Sefton, out, Boyer walking with him, and they're still talking. Seem to have hit on something in common."

5

It was a very thoughtful Boyer who joined Slade and the sheriff a little later. He hitched his chair close and spoke in low tones.

"Sefton put a proposition up to me," he said. "I figure it to be rather attractive, but I want your opinion, Mr. Slade. You know the Circle C ranch is for sale. Tim Ester is moving west to a place he bought over there. Already sent his cows and his hands over to his new holding. Will follow them as soon as he disposes of the Circle C. Sefton has an option on the place, but he hasn't enough money to meet Ester's asking price. So he suggested to me that I go in with him and we'll take over the spread on halves. He says it's just a matter of time till the land is worth a lot more than we'll be paying for it. I feel sorta that way about it myself. What do you think, Mr. Slade?"

"I'd say," the Ranger replied without

hesitancy, "that if his option is strictly in order and he puts in his money without delay that it will be a good investment, a very good investment."

"If that's how you feel about it, I'll tell Sefton okay. Would you look over the papers when they're ready, Mr. Slade?"

"Be glad to," Slade answered.

"Now I feel fine about it," chuckled Boyer. "Let's all have a drink."

After the glasses were empty and Boyer had returned to the far end of the bar, Slade turned to Calder and lowered his voice.

"Tom," he said, "I can tell you what I couldn't tell Boyer, the matter being a dead secret, or supposed to be. You know General Manager Jaggers Dunn of the great C. & P. Railroad System is building a line west to the Winter Gardens. Everybody knows that. What is not generally known, Mr. Dunn also plans to build a line south here to link with the Mexican railroad. And he'll want to build his assembly yard on the Circle E land and will be glad to pay a very hefty sum for the section of the Circle E he'll need. So it looks like Boyer is all set to cash in nicely on his investment. Which goes for Sefton also."

"Rumhole owners always get the breaks," snorted Calder. "Oh, well, Boyer never seems to spend much money, but he gives away plenty. He's always an easy touch. Guess he deserves a break now and then. Let's drink!"

Which they proceeded to do. Boyer sent over another snort for the sheriff, coffee for Slade.

"Well, we've been clear around Robin Hood's barn, as the saying goes, and right back where we started from," the sheriff remarked. "No notion who to suspect, no notion where the devils will hit next."

"At least we have a good list of possibilities," Slade replied cheerfully. Calder grunted and did not look impressed.

"And what's the next move?" he asked. Slade was silent for a few moments, then,

"I think I'll go over to the bank and have a talk with Charley Clint, the president. "After closing hours, but I imagine he'll open up for me. And he might have something to tell us."

"That's a notion," Calder agreed. "He's been a help before."

Arriving at the bank, Slade had no difficulty gaining admission. The president, an old friend, had a warm greeting for him. He sent for coffee and they settled down to talk.

"What's on your mind, Walt?" the president asked.

"Charley," the Ranger replied, "is there any money coming in today from outlying parts, by stage, or train, or some other type of conveyance?"

"Nope," said Clint, "but there's some going out."

"Yes?" Slade was at once interested. "How's that?"

"There's a hefty sum leaving here for Port Isabel on the 11:15 tonight. A fellow down there plans to build a large apartment house and wants cash for certain goods he can get at a bargain. I recall we discussed that plan when you were here before and you advised him to go ahead and build to take care of the tourist trade that is steadily mounting at Port Isabel, attracted by the excellent fishing to be had in the vicinity. Well, he's taking your advice and going ahead with his building."

"I see," Slade said. "And I suppose it is a secret that the money will be on the 11:15?"

The banker chuckled. "Supposed to be," he replied. "But the characters we have been getting hereabouts of late seem able to learn anything they want to, no matter how secret it is supposed to be."

"And the train will be in the yards until leaving time," Slade remarked thoughtfully.

"That's right," answered Clint. "It always is."

"And the money will be in the express car safe?"

"Right again. You think the devils might make a play for that money?"

"I deem it not beyond the realm of possibility," Slade said.

"The yard police are guarding the train," Clint pointed out.

"Yes, while it is in the yards, but not after it leaves Brownsville for Port Isabel."

"By gosh! You're right there," exclaimed the president. "So if the hellions do make a try for the money, it'll be somewhere between here and Port Isabel?"

"That's what my hunch tells me," Slade replied.

"And as we all know, your hunches are mighty apt to be straight ones," said Clint. "Anything I can do to help?"

"You've helped a lot already," Slade told him. "But there is one thing you can do. Have old Pete, your night watchman, ease over into the yards after dark and tell Horton, the night yardmaster, to slip into the sheriff's office about nine o'clock. He's reliable, and so is old Pete. They'll know better than to make it obvious, if anybody happens to be keeping tabs on them, which I figure is highly unlikely."

"I'll do it," the banker promised.

"Thanks, Charley, be seeing you," Slade said.

Slade wasted no time getting back to the sheriff's office and acquainting Calder with what he had planned.

"By gosh! I believe it'll work," the sheriff enthused. "And we might even bag the big he-wolf of the pack. With as nice a haul as that *dinero* would make, I'd say he's likely to handle that one in person."

"Possibly," Slade conceded. "Now we'll slide across the bridge to Amado's cantina and line up Estevan. He's just the man for this chore."

"Or any chore that promises action and a chance for that thirsty blade of his to knock off a drink. Let's go!"

They found Estevan at the cantina. His black eyes snapped and sparkled as Slade outlined his plan, and he caressed the haft of his knife, lovingly.

"Another spell of nail-biting for me," sighed Dolores. "Oh, well, I no longer worry too much. You always come out —"

"On top!" the sheriff interpolated, with a chuckle. Dolores favored him with a disdainful look, and refused to rise to the bait.

It was close to sundown and they enjoyed

a leisurely dinner while waiting for it to get dark.

"We won't leave town until after nine or a little later," Slade explained. "We'll get back to the office in time to line up Deputy Webley for his chore. Then ride."

They talked together for a while. Slade and Dolores danced several numbers. Amado insisted they partake of a final glass of his favorite wine. Slade glanced at the clock, patted Dolores' hand, and stood up.

"The roses will be waiting, and so will I," she said. "Take care of yourself, darling." Her anxious eyes followed him to the swinging doors.

When they reached the office, they found Webley awaiting them, the light turned very low. With him was Horton, the night general yardmaster, to whom Slade gave some very explicit instructions. Horton listened closely, then said:

"Everything will be taken care of, Mr. Slade, and I'll be right there to make sure. You go right ahead, you'll get plumb perfect cooperation. Good luck!" He slid out the door and made for the dark yard and the spur on which the train stood before rolling to the station. Twenty minutes later, the posse rode west on the river trail.

As they rode, Slade constantly scanned

the back track, although he had little fear they would be followed. However, best not to take chances with so shrewd an outfit opposed to him. After a couple of miles had been covered, and Santa Rita was but a short distance ahead, he gave an order and the horses were turned and sent at a fast pace back the way they had come. Not until they were in the shadow of a thicket close to the yards did he draw rein. He, Estevan, and the sheriff dismounted. Webley remained in his hull, holding the horses' bridles.

"Okay," Slade told him. "Wait till the train pulls out from the station, then go ahead and stable the cayuses and hole up in the office, where we can get in touch with you by wire should the need arise."

"Right!" said the deputy. "Good hunting!"

For some minutes, Slade stood studying the shadowy yard. On the nearby spur stood the Port Isabel train, engine purring softly.

"I think this move should fool anybody who might have been keeping tabs on our moves in town," he said to his companions, speaking very low. "I'm counting on them believing that we are headed west to investigate something that has been reported. I figure they will fall for it, and if so, everything should work out in a satisfactory manner. Now listen close; here's the layout of the express car:

"The express car safe is toward the rear of the car. With the light low, as it will be, the front of the car, next to the engine, will be quite shadowy, and that's where we will be, with the light in our favor. If they do make a try for the money, they'll come in by way of the rear door, next to the coaches. Door is supposed to be locked, but that will pose no difficulty to such a bunch, they'll get in all right, and get the drop on the messenger and order him to open the safe. That will be your cue, Tom, to announce us. Being law enforcement officers, we must give them a chance to surrender. They won't, you can count on that, so shoot fast and shoot straight. We'll very likely be outnumbered, but with conditions being what they will be, I figure the odds won't be too lopsided. Everything understood, now? Okay, ten more minutes and we move."

The ten minutes dragged by on leaden feet, or so it seemed to the waiting posse. Finally, however, Slade breathed, "Let's go!" and led the way, peering and listening, to the front of the express car. As they reached it, Horton, the yardmaster, loomed from the darkness between the car and the engine tender.

"All set," he whispered. "Everything taken care of. Messenger knows just what to do; he's dependable. Nobody been hanging around."

Without wasting time to speak, Slade patted his shoulder and eased up the steps to the "blind baggage," as the space between tender and car is called in railroad parlance. Estevan and the sheriff crowded close behind him. He tapped lightly on the door and it swung open. Silently, they glided into the car, the express messenger closing the door behind them. He was a rugged-looking elderly individual and Slade believed Horton was right, that he was dependable. He proceeded to give him some precise orders.

"If the devils do show, don't argue, do exactly as they tell you to," he said. "When the shooting starts, I'm pretty sure it will, hit the floor and stay there."

"Think they're going to wreck the train?" the messenger asked apprehensively.

"Nothing so crude as that, I would say," Slade replied. "Then there would be a chance that the express car would be turned over, the doors jammed. No, they'll come in through the back door, quietly, loot the safe and then stop the train at some spot where horses will be held waiting for them. That's the way I figure it, and I believe I'm right."

71

The messenger nodded his understanding.

The engine sounded two short whistle blasts, the exhaust boomed and the train rolled out of the yards and ground to a halt at the station. There followed the usual turmoil and bustle that attends a departing train.

Gradually the shouting stilled. The engine bell began clanging. Two more short whistle blasts and the 11:15 rolled toward Port Isabel.

"Now we can just take it easy and await developments," Slade said, speaking in normal tones, there being no danger of being heard above the roar and rattle of the train. He squatted comfortably against the wall, rolled and lighted a cigarette and smoked placidly.

The others were not quite so blasé, casting frequent glances toward the rear door.

The miles flowed back under the turning wheels. Slade estimated the distance covered and became a trifle more alert. Any time now, he figured. But still the train sped on, and nothing happened. And gradually *El Halcón* experienced a growing uneasiness and began to wonder if his hunch was a straight one after all. It really began to look that way. At the moment, the train was passing through a long and very narrow cut, with just enough room for the tracks, and little to spare, between the steep sides, some of them brush-grown. Beyond the cut was very likely where the attempt would be made, he figured. What happened next proved that even *El Halcón* could sometimes figure wrong.

6

Suddenly the booming exhaust snapped off. There was a scream of tortured metal as the brake shoes ground against the tires. The big engine leaped and bucked. The express car swayed wildly. The messenger and the posse were thrown off their feet and sent scooting along the floor.

A terrific crash! The express car rocked and reeled, and brought up leaning against the side of the cut. It did not turn over.

"Back this way!" Slade shouted, scrambling to his feet. "Make for the front door. Keep away from that side door!"

The others obeyed. They reached the front door. As Slade seized the knob and tore it open, there was a thunderous explosion. The side door flew to pieces.

"Dynamite! Threw dynamite!" Slade snapped as they whisked down the slanting steps to the ground.

Six men were racing from the brush, heading for the shattered door, one shooting at the coach windows.

"Up!" bawled the sheriff. "In the name of the law!"

The white blur of turning faces! A blaze of shots as Slade fired with both hands! The light was very bad; it was almost blind shooting. But one outlaw plunged to the ground. Estevan's knife buzzed through the air and another fell, screaming hoarsely.

Answering bullets slammed into the side of the car, caromed off the steel side of the tender. One grazed Slade's forehead, sending red flashes before his eyes, hurling him sideways with the shock. He recovered, squeezed triggers again and again, and still again. A third outlaw fell. Estevan and the sheriff were shooting, with no results, for through the powder fog there was practically no light.

A deep and resonant voice bellowed an order. The forms of the three remaining outlaws were but flickering shadows into the brush that clothed the side of the cut. The hammers of Slade's Colts clicked on empty shells. He dashed forward, reloading with smooth speed. A slug struck the heel of his boot, throwing him off balance and to the ground. The sheriff fell over his prostrate form. Estevan, swearing in three languages, managed to dodge both but lost precious seconds of time.

From the crest of the cut slope sounded a beat of fast hoofs, fading into the distance.

"Hold it!" Slade gasped. "They're gone!" Still considerably shaken by the hard fall, he managed to get to his feet and reach down a hand to the floundering and cursing sheriff, helping him to rise.

"Anybody hurt?" Slade asked anxiously.

"Guess not," said the old messenger. "I got my gun trained on those three devils on the ground, 'gainst the chance they might be playin' possum."

"Don't think you need worry, from the looks of them," Slade replied. "Slip into the car and light all the lamps and turn them high. Bring one out here so we can look them over. And I'm apologizing to you for the stupid remark I made, that they wouldn't wreck the train. The shrewd hellions staged it where the car would fall on the inside of the curve and couldn't turn over because of the close supporting side of the cut."

"You did all right," said the messenger. "Saved the money, did for three skunks. A fine night's work. I'll get the lamp."

The coaches were a bedlam of yells and screams and weird profanity, the passengers

76

pouring out. The blue-clad conductor, lantern in hand, came hurrying forward.

"My God, Sheriff, what happened?" he asked.

"See if the engineer and fireman are all right," Slade told him. "The way they're swearing, I don't think they're injured to any serious extent, but make sure."

In fact, the enginemen were already out of their cab and on the ground, rubbing superficial bruises.

"Were slowing for the curve and didn't hit that pile of cross-ties too hard," said the engineer. "Played hell with the front of the engine, though."

Slade examined the front of the engine and decided that aside from the smashed pilot, it had not suffered any appreciable damage. But it would take a crane to right the derailed express car. He turned to the conductor.

"Have you a portable telegraph instrument aboard?" he asked.

"Yep, we've got one, but I don't know about hooking it up; those poles are mighty high," he said dubiously.

"Fetch the instrument and I'll hook it up," Slade said.

A little later the conductor shook his head. "Goin' up that pole like a squirrel!" he

77

marvelled. "Is there anything that young feller can't do?"

"Maybe," replied Sheriff Calder, "but if so, nobody has found it out yet. You know him, don't you?"

"Sure, your special deputy, Mr. Slade," said the conductor. "Guess everybody knows that."

In a matter of minutes the instrument was hooked up.

"You can send?" Slade called down from his lofty perch. "If you can't, I can."

"I can tap out enough to let Brownsville and Port Isabel know what happened," the conductor shouted back.

"And tell Brownsville I said to send us transportation back to town with the bodies," Slade directed.

The conductor got busy with the key. "All set," he called a little later. Slade threw down the extension wires and descended, to find Calder and the express messenger regaling the assembled passengers, none of whom were seriously injured, with a vivid account of just what had happened — highly colored, Slade thought. He was favored with admiring glances, especially on the part of several ladies present. Finally he managed to escape by means of the pretext to locate the horses ridden by the dead outlaws, Estevan assisting.

Without difficulty they found them, tethered to tree branches. The rigs were removed and the horses were turned loose to fend for themselves until picked up.

Slade wasted little more than a cursory glance on the dead outlaws, one with a throat neatly sliced by a "thirsty" blade. He would examine them more closely in the office. Typical border scum with nothing outstanding about them, he told Calder.

The passengers speculated on them with much conjecture, several mantaining vaguely that they had seen one or the other in Brownsville, to which Slade gave little thought.

"And again the head man made good his escape," he remarked to the sheriff. "Oh, that was he, all right, who bellowed the order to hightail."

"His time will come," Calder predicted confidently.

Horton, the Brownsville general yardmaster, was right on the job, and little more than an hour had passed when the wreck train arrived, following it a light engine and a caboose for the accommodation of the posse and the bodies. Ready volunteers helped load the bodies and the little train chug-chugged for Brownsville, arriving at the river town well before daylight.

Horton had men ready to convey the bodies to the sheriff's office, where Slade and Calder gave them a careful once-over.

"This time all three were once cowhands," *El Halcón* said. "But not for quite some time; marks of rope and branding iron are fading out."

"They'd have done better to stick to following a cow's tail," the sheriff grunted. "Guess orneriness is born in a man and sooner or later it crops out. A nice passel of *dinero* in their pockets. Here, Estevan, your boys deserve a mite of celebration. The rest will pay for planting the scuts. Doc can hold one of his darn fool inquests on them, then away to Boot Hill. Now what?"

"The Blue Bell and a bite to eat, and then bed," Slade replied.

When they reached the saloon, they were not surprised to find Dolores awaiting them, Boyer keeping her company. Otherwise the Blue Bell was closed for the night.

"Knew you'd be stopping here first," the girl said. "So I rode across the bridge, a couple of Estevan's *amigos* riding herd on me. Now tell me just what happened.

"Never a dull moment," she sighed after the sheriff had finished his account of the business. "Well, everybody will be singing

80

your praises tomorrow. Nice to be famous, but hard on those who have to stand on the sidelines and wait." She glanced at the clock.

"Now you've really made a start," the sheriff remarked to Slade the following afternoon as they sat in the office and contemplated the blanketed forms on the floor. "Outfigured the hellions for fair. Kept them from making a whopping big haul and cut down on their number by three."

"I'm not particularly proud of the episode," Slade said. "It seems to me that I was very neatly outfigured. I sure failed to call the turn when I told the messenger that I was confident the devils would not wreck the train."

"Results are what count, and you sure got results," Calder returned. "Keep on falling down that way and the chore will mighty soon be finished. But blast it! We still haven't any notion as to who is the head sidewinder of the nest."

"Yes," Slade agreed. "About all we have to go on, and not definitely, is that he appears to be a big tall jigger, and we could be wrong at that."

"Uh-huh, but now and then I get to thinking of a big tall jigger who seems to sorta fill the bill."

"Okay, but don't go thinking out loud," Slade repeated a former remark. "You might be doing somebody an injustice. Something I've pointed out before, if you'll recall, when a mite of thinking out loud would have wronged somebody."

"Oh, sure, I'll keep a tight latigo on my jaw," promised Calder. "But I figure I've got a right to think to myself."

"Definitely," Slade smiled.

"Now what?" asked the sheriff. Slade glanced out the window at the flood of golden sunshine.

"Now," he said, "I think I'll take a little stroll while waiting for Doc to show up with his coroner's jury to hold an inquest on those specimens. I'll be back before he arrives."

"And watch your step," Calder cautioned. "You must be mighty, mighty unpopular in certain quarters about now, and the devils have shown they'll go to any lengths to drop a loop on you. So have a care."

"I'll have a care," Slade replied carelessly. "Would be nice if the head man is so riled over what happened last night that he'll pay me a visit in person. Might tend to simplify matters."

The sheriff gave a disgusted snort and turned to the papers on his desk. Slade chuckled and sauntered out.

As he walked, Slade pondered the future of this town at the southernmost tip of the United States, already the largest city in the Lower Rio Grande Valley. He believed it had a future of greatness. There was everything to make it so. Undoubtedly it would be a winter resort, with its average annual temperature of 73 degrees. Gulf breezes in the summer and warm sunshine in winter would make year-round sports possible. Salt water fishing in the Gulf of Mexico was only about twenty-five miles distant. Duck and goose shooting and wild game hunting in the outlying brush country would attract, was attracting already, sportsmen from all parts of the country. There would be beach resorts, golf and boating to offer a diversity of recreation.

Through centuries the Rio Grande had deposited silt that would make Brownsville the center of a rich delta of citrus orchards, vegetable farms and cotton fields. Already irrigation was converting the surrounding region into an oasis, green all through the year, that would make possible the city's greatest wealth.

Yes, Walt Slade firmly believed that Brownsville was a town with a future. He could envision residential areas of beautiful homes set in spacious grounds and aflame with the brilliant blossoms of scarlet and purple bougainvillea and other tropical and sub-tropical flowers.

And he thrilled to the thought that he might be able to play a part in this development of beauty and content. For before the city could really come into its own, outlawry must be banished. Well, Fate, employing Captain Jim McNelty as an instrument, had assigned him that chore; he'd do his best. He walked on with a carefree mind.

It was a beautiful day, the sky its deepest sun-washed blue, with just enough of a breeze to temper the heat. So beautiful that Slade experienced a growing urge for the quiet and peace of the open trail trending on to the ever-retreating horizon. Abruptly he turned and retraced his steps to the sheriff's office.

"I'm going to take a little ride west," he announced. Calder regarded him suspiciously.

"Got something in mind?" he asked. Slade shook his head.

"Certainly nothing definite; just feel the notion. And remember once before I took a ride just because I felt that way, with good results."

"And came nigh to getting yourself

drygulched," the sheriff reminded. "Don't hanker for company?"

"I really can't see the need," El Halcón replied. "I know you've got a lot of paper work to catch up. Get it over with against when something really important comes along to interrupt."

"Okay," said Calder, turning back to his paper-littered desk.

Making his way to the stable, Slade cinched up, chatted with old Agosto, the keeper, and then rode up Jefferson Street to the river trail, turning west. Soon Santa Rita hove into view, a sparse scattering of ancient adobes, the majority of them uninhabited, basking in the fading glory of an almost-forgotten name. For here once was a seat of power, whence Juan Nepomuceno (Cheno) Cartinas, the red scourge of the Rio Grande, directed his raids. But United States troops and the Rangers drove Cartinas back to Mexico where, a national hero in the eyes of his people, he ended his days as Governor of the Mexican State of Tamaulipas.

Yes, power is ever-fleeting, elusive as "a feather is wafted downward from an eagle in his flight," Slade reflected as he gazed on the vestige of departed grandeur. He rode on.

La Paloma was drowsy and sun-baked,

like an old *peon* wrapped in his *serape* and content to let the world go by. Los Indios was somewhat livelier, with a few people actually moving about and with hands to wave to the lone horseman, greetings that Slade returned. An elderly Mexican recognized *El Halcón* and bowed low. Slade acknowledged the bow, his cold eyes abruptly all kindness, and flashed the white smile of *El Halcón,* leaving the old fellow beaming.

Santa Maria appeared oblivious to the ceaseless clang of the huge pump lifting water from the river to irrigation ditches. Here there were prosperous farms and orchards. He passed Taylor Ross' grape arbors. Ross was not in evidence at the moment and Slade did not linger, for he did not wish his ride to be interrupted.

Several barren miles followed — no farms. Then Progresso, where Slade did not pause. A couple more miles and he slowed Shadow's gait. Now he was passing over the Circle C holding, that Fats Boyer and the lawyer and land speculator, Vibart Sefton, planned to buy. The spread was very long, south to north, but rather narrow, east to west. It was the last ranch west for many miles, the land beyond being very heavily brush-grown and quite arid.

Slade slowed to a walk, for he wished to study the spread. Yes, the south pastures would be ideal for the C. & P. assembly yard. Boyer was making a good investment.

He gazed at the nearby river. "A first-class ford across the Rio Grande here," he remarked to Shadow. "Which is interesting. And not so very far to the west, on the south bank, is the quite lively Mexican town of Ciudad Camargo, which is also interesting. Beginning to get a hunch, horse, a sorta loco one, but a hunch. Well, we'll see. No telling how things will work out, and perhaps soon."

For some space the view to the north had been obscured by a thick and high stand of chaparral, but the trail climbed steeply to a level crest that was free from growth. Slade glanced to the north and his interest quickened.

A man was riding down from the north. Slade gazed at the approaching horseman, wondering who he might be, for all of Ester's hands had already departed to their new holding far to the west, where Ester would join them as soon as his deal with Boyer and Sefton was consummated. And the approaching rider was certainly not chunky old Tim.

And then, a few minutes later, as the

horseman drew near the trail, Slade leaned forward in the hull, his face wearing an expression of surprise. For in the oncoming rider he had recognized Mostyn Selby, whose saloon, the Albemarle, had been held up and robbed. Now what in blazes was he doing on the Circle C spread? Perhaps *he* had a deal with Ester in mind. Sheriff Calder had intimated that he appeared to be pretty well heeled. Probably Boyer and Sefton had gotten under the wire just in time.

Slade wondered if Selby recognized him. Very likely, for as he reached the trail, he waved his hand in a cordial fashion. Slade returned the greeting.

However, Selby did not head in his direction, but turned east on the trail at a fast pace. Slade shrugged his shoulders and turned his attention elsewhere.

Sunset was flaming in the west. Before long it would be full dark. He rode a couple more miles and after a final glance around he turned Shadow's nose east and headed for town.

"And if you're as hungry as I am, you won't waste any time getting there," he told the horse. "Going to be long past nosebag time the best you can do. And Calder is going to be snorting, wondering where the blankety-blank-blank we've gotten to, and into what."

Shadow blew cheerful agreement, and quickened his pace. Slade let him set his own gait; it had been a long day of steady slogging, even for Shadow.

7

The vivid hues in the west had faded and the blue dusk was sifting down from the hilltops. Very quickly now it would be full dark. Slade became more alert, carefully studying his surroundings as he rode. This was a lonely trail, where anything could happen. He did not think that anybody had followed him from town, keeping well back out of sight, knowing he must return this way to reach Brownsville — but it would be foolish to ignore the possibility. Once he had come unpleasantly close to riding into a drygulching on this trail, some distance farther east. History could repeat itself.

Progresso was mostly dark and quiet and Slade did not pause, although the lights of a saloon winked invitingly. A bite to eat wouldn't go bad, but he could wait until reaching Brownsville and then take his time over a leisurely meal.

There was neither light nor movement

around Taylor Ross' grape arbors. Santa Maria was also quiet, save for the ceaseless clamor of the pump.

Los Indios showed a few lights, not many. Oil lamps and flickering tallow wicks stood in the windows of homes and store buildings, with an occasional soft glow where family cooking was being done over charcoal braziers in the yards.

La Paloma was more subdued. Slade breathed a sigh of relief. Only a few more miles, then Santa Rita and Brownsville and something to eat, which he was feeling more in need of.

A golden moon had risen in the east and soon the landscape was almost as bright as day, and the Ranger's vigilance increased, especially when the trail climbed a slope that leveled off at the crest, where he knew he would be visible for some distance. But he reached the far downward slope without incident. It looked like his unease was unjustified — for the moment.

Highly developed in *El Halcón* was that peculiar instinct, a subtle sixth sense that warns of danger when none, apparently, is present, something he had learned long before not to ignore. And abruptly the voiceless monitor was storming in his brain. Another moment and a sound of maudlin singing reached his ears. Sounded like somebody had looked upon the wine when it was red and various other colors. The decidedly unmusical racket loudened. Around a bend directly ahead loomed two horsemen, bawling their darndest, one brandishing a bottle. Slade started to chuckle, then abruptly desisted, his eyes narrowing.

The bottle-waver let out a whoop, "Howdy, cowboy! Have a drink with us?" Slade shook his head.

"Oh, well, if you won't, you won't," said the other. "And there really ain't but a wee drapie left." They swept past, still singing.

Without warning Slade sent Shadow toward the brush that flanked the trail. He plunged from the saddle as two guns blazed.

"Got him!" a voice howled exultantly. "He —"

The voice was drowned by a rattling crash of Slade's Colts as, prone, snugged against the brush, he shot with both hands.

One of the "drunks" whirled from his hull to thud in the dust of the trail. Answering slugs whined over Slade's prostrate form.

Again the boom of the big forty-fives, and there were two riderless horses snorting up the trail.

For a moment Slade lay flat, guns trained

on the two motionless forms. Then he reloaded his Colts and stood up, listening.

No further sound broke the moonlit stillness. Looked like there were no more of the devils about. He stood up, holstering his irons.

"A very neat try, feller, strictly original," he remarked to Shadow, who looked bored by the whole affair. "Yes, a very neat try, and they might have gotten by with it if they hadn't made the little slip their brand seems always to make. Never do I recall seeing drunks with hatbrims drawn low, neckerchiefs looped up high. That's not the normal reaction to redeye in large quantities. So naturally I was all of a sudden a bit suspicious. Yes, the little slip, and in this case as there on the bridge, fatal."

He gave the bodies a quick once-over, decided there was nothing outstanding shown by either, although he did feel that they had been well above the average of intelligence.

"But I don't think they figured this attempt on their own," he told Shadow. "Well, we'll leave them where they are. Somebody will be reporting them to the sheriff. Best that way, I figure; may puzzle somebody, which will be all to the good. The horses are to heck and gone so we won't bother our heads about them; somebody will pick them up. So let's make another try for town before we topple over from hunger."

Reaching Brownsville without further mishap, Slade first cared for his horse. Old Agosto, the stable keeper, was still up and around and at once took care of the big black, providing him with everything needful, including a good rubdown.

Knowing his mount would lack for nothing, Slade repaired to the Blue Bell, where he found the sheriff fortified by a full glass.

"And where the devil have you been for the past fifteen or sixteen hours, and what you been into?" he demanded accusingly.

Slade told him, in detail. Calder indulged in some vivid profanity.

"And another try at doing you in, eh?" he growled.

"And another failure," Slade replied. "Really, it's getting monotonous."

The sheriff rumbled disgustedly. "Well, if Selby had it in mind to tie onto the Circle C, he was too late," he remarked. "Boyer will have the papers for you to look over tomorrow. They're all signed and rarin' to go. Tim will be headed west in another day or so.

"Incidentally," he added, "Dolores sent word she'd be riding over here, and said to wait for her. I expect her any minute, Estevan with her. Estevan is going to be plumb out of temper, missing out on another chance to give his knife a drink. Oh, well, I figure he'll have plenty of opportunities before this business is finished. Here comes your dinner; get on the outside of it."

Slade proceeded to do so. Before he had finished eating, Dolores and Estevan arrived, the girl relieved to find him still all in one piece, Estevan decidedly disgruntled when he learned what he had missed.

"Tomorrow we'll have another little talk, after somebody has reported finding a couple of dead men in the trail west of Santa Rita," Slade said.

8

When Slade arrived at the sheriff's office, around mid-afternoon, he found the bodies of the two drygulchers neatly laid out on the floor, Calder regarding the blanketed forms with serene satisfaction.

"A couple of Zeke Combs' hands were ridin' to town and found them," Calder explained. "They hightailed to tell me about it. So Webley and Gus rounded up a couple of pack mules and we fetched 'em in. Ornery-lookin' scuts."

"About average," Slade replied. "Anybody recall seeing them in town?"

"Oh, same old story, two or three bartenders sure they served them at one time or another. Didn't remember anything about them," the sheriff answered. He chuckled.

"Beat you to it this time," he said. "I took a look at their hands; both were cowhands a long time back. Now what you got in mind?"

Slade countered with a question of his own, "Any widelooping of late?"

"Ain't none been reported for better'n a week," Calder replied. "Maybe you've scared 'em off."

"Not likely," Slade differed. "None for a week or more, eh?"

"That's right. You getting a notion of some sort?"

Slade did not reply at once but gazed out the window, his eyes thoughtful. Calder waited patiently, knowing *El Halcón* would talk when ready, and not before. Finally Slade turned from the window.

"Tom," he said, "I'm getting a hunch. Perhaps a sort of loco one, but I've a feeling it's worth playing. We have nothing to lose except perhaps some sleep."

"We'll play it, and I betcha it gets results," the sheriff declared.

"Feel up to riding the river trail tonight to the Circle C spread?" Slade asked.

"Sure," Calder instantly responded. "You figure something will be pulled there?"

"As conditions are now, the Circle C is a widelooper's happy dream," Slade replied. "Not a soul on the holding, no patrols. Run a herd west from Lanham's or Combs' north pastures, which are never well guarded, to the Circle C and then a straight

97

shoot to an excellent ford, across the river to Mexico. Perfect!"

"Darned if it don't sound like you've hit on something," enthused the sheriff. "Anyhow, we'll sure play it. Might bag the whole nest of sidewinders, maybe even the top snake."

"At least we might be able to give the outfit a really severe jolt," Slade said.

"No doubt about that," agreed Calder. "And they've already gotten a few of late. That pair's pockets coughed up quite a bit of money. Imagine it would have been a lot more if they'd gotten by with the train robbery."

"Yes, losing that haul must have hurt," Slade nodded. "Which is to a certain extent the basis of my hunch. I figure the head of the outfit needs to replenish his exchequer, and cows always provide a quick turnover."

Calder glanced out the window. "Here comes Doc with his coroner's jury to set on those rapscallions. Shouldn't take long, seeing he has no witnesses to call. He may do a mite of shrewd guessing, but guessing doesn't go at an inquest."

The sheriff was right. The inquest was a speedy affair, 'lowing that the deceased met their death at the hands of parties unknown, or perhaps at the hand of each other. A rider to the verdict opined that from the looks of them, the community hadn't lost much. Plant 'em and forget 'em. Court adjourned.

"And now what's the next move?" Calder asked, after the coroner and his jury had departed and the bodies had been packed off to Boot Hill.

"I believe you said the deputies would be here soon after the inquest," Slade replied. "Tell them to ride west shortly before dark, to turn off at the track that leads to Zeke Combs' casa. Ride slowly and as soon as it begins to get dark, turn back and hole up in the big thicket close to where the Combs track joins the river trail, and wait for us to show. You and I and Estevan won't leave town until after dark. I doubt if anyone will follow us out of town. Doesn't really matter if somebody does, for they can't get ahead of us. I sincerely doubt the hellions will divine that we have figured out the Circle C advantages and will make a play for them there. I'm working on the premise that the move will catch them completely by surprise. Hope so, anyhow."

"I think it will," Calder said. "Suppose you'll be dropping over to Amado's cantina to line up Estevan?"

"That's right," Slade answered. "I figure he has a right to be in on this."

99

"He sure has," the sheriff agreed. "He'd feel bad if he was left out. Besides, he's a mighty strong stick to lean on when the going gets rough. They don't come any better. Okay, be seeing you at the Blue Bell a bit before dark. Better line our bellies before we start out."

When he reached the cantina, Slade found Estevan in his usual place at the near end of the bar. A flashing white grin brightened his dark face when Slade told him what was planned. Dolores saw it and shook her curly head resignedly.

"I know that look," she said. "It means trouble."

"Trouble for others, not for *Capitán,*" Estevan replied. "He the on top out always comes."

"And will somebody please unscramble that one," Dolores sighed. "But any way you phrase it, it means trouble for me."

"If things work out tonight as I expect them to, we may have a few days of peace and quiet for a change," Slade reassured her.

"We can stand a few, and more than a few," she said. "Oh well, I guess Estevan has the right of it. On with the dance! Let joy be unconfined!"

They had several numbers on the floor,

and a glass of wine together. With the flashing blue of the sky deepening to glowing purple, Slade crossed the bridge to the Blue Bell.

"Let us eat!" said the sheriff.

They proceeded to do so. Then after a smoke, they made their way to Agosto's stable, where they found Estevan and his wiry mustang awaiting them. They cinched up and rode west at a fast pace on the river trail.

Slade watched the back track for a while and saw no indications of their being followed. He faced to the front and increased the pace a little more, slowing as they neared the track that ran down from Zeke Combs' casa. Webley and Gus rode from the nearby thicket to join them and they proceeded west.

Los Indios, Santa Maria, Taylor Ross' grape arbors, Progresso, and Dixon Lanham's holding fell back under the horses' drumming irons, and Slade grew watchful; for in a few miles they would be on the Circle C land. He constantly searched the terrain ahead with eyes that missed nothing, as they neared the ford. Needed was a spot where they could hole up and see without being seen — and not too far from the ford, that was imperative.

Also, there was an unpleasant contingency that had to be reckoned with: it was just possible that the shrewd devil the outlaws were lurking near the ford, waiting to mow who headed the bunch had anticipated their move and that them down when they appeared. Slade believed he had that angle taken care of, but was not altogether sure.

So it was with a breath of relief that he sighted what he had noted the night before, a quite long stand of thick and tall chaparral that fringed the crest of the slope, dropped down to the water's edge and extended to the ford and beyond. The configuration of the terrain was such that riders approaching from the east could not be seen until they came quite close to the narrow track that ran through the brush and down to the ford.

The moon was up, but a film of cloud wrack dimmed its light, and close to the brush shadows predominated. It wasn't very good shooting light, but it would help to veil their approach.

They reached the beginning of the belt of growth. A little farther and Slade called a halt.

"Keep your voices down," he cautioned. "Here we leave the horses, in the brush; can't risk their clumping any longer."

The horses were effectually concealed, all but Shadow tethered to tree trunks. His split reins were just dropped to the ground, all that was necessary to keep him put until called for. Slade stood at the edge of the growth, gazing northward, his eyes thoughtful.

A routine procedure, everything going smoothly, like those he had taken part in before. Hole up in the brush and wait for the wideloopers to show. Very simple.

But suppose the outlaws had anticipated his move and were holed up near the ford waiting for *him* to show? The results might be highly unpleasant. Abruptly he arrived at a decision.

"Stay here and keep very quiet," he told his companions. "I'll be seeing you shortly." Ignoring the sheriff's mumbled protest, he slipped into the brush and glided west toward the ford.

Utterly silent, he eased along, careful to tread on no dry and fallen branch, to dislodge no stone and set it rolling.

As he neared the ford, his caution increased and he barely crept along, pausing often to peer and listen. Now the ford was uncomfortably close and still no sound broke the stillness save the gurgling of the river as it chafed its banks.

And then he froze in his tracks. From directly ahead came a mutter of low voices, little more than whispers. His hunch was a straight one — the outlaws were there, waiting! When the cows arrived, they would stream down the track through the brush, the riders bunched behind them. That would be the sheriff's cue to announce himself, being required as a law enforcement officer to give the devils their undeserved chance to surrender to the posse.

But the posse would never have a chance. The outlaws holed up in the brush, guns trained, would instantly open fire. A very, very clever scheme that would have worked were it not for *El Halcón*'s wise foresight.

For long moments, Slade stood motionless, thinking hard. Finally he believed he had arrived at a solution that should turn the tables on the devils. That is, if he could only make it work.

The weak link in the chain was the deputies. Estevan would move through the growth like a wraith, and Calder also was good at brush work. But the deputies, brave, dependable men though they were, might well make the slight noise that would warn the outlaws of their presence.

Well, he would have to risk it and hope for the best. He could think of no alternative. Soundlessly, he made his way back to his companions. After telling them what he had in mind, he concluded to the deputies,

"So when we start moving, try and step where I step. Test the ground with your foot before putting your weight upon it. Keep your heads down going under branches. Everything depends on our getting set without being discovered. Succeed in that and I believe the scheme will work."

"You're darn right it will," muttered Calder. "Should throw the hellions completely off balance, and that's all we need. Did you get any notion as to how many are holed up down there?"

"I judge about four," Slade replied. "I can't say for certain, but I'm confident there are not more than four. We'll be outnumbered, all right, but the element of surprise on which we can count should sort of even the score. Now all we can do is wait for the cows to show, which should be soon; it's past midnight. No more talking now, against the chance one of the devils might be nosing around."

The wait was tedious, but not too long. Less than half an hour had passed when Slade saw, far to the north, the moving shadow that he knew to be the herd of wide-looped cows.

"Quite a bunch of them, too," he whispered. "Looks like well over a hundred head."

"I can't see anything," whisper-grumbled Calder. "Them eyes of yours!"

"You will in a minute or two," Slade breathed, his eyes estimating the distance the cattle had to cover to reach the ford, and the time it would take them at the rate they were traveling. He tensed for action.

"Five riders shoving them," he whispered. "Okay, here we go!"

Through the tangle of growth he led the way, the deputies close behind him, Calder and Estevan bringing up the rear. More than once Slade held his breath as a deputy foot floundered slightly. But now the bawling cows, their hoofs pounding the soil, were close, and he believed the attention of the holed-up outlaws would be directed to the herd for the moment and a slight sound wouldn't be likely to impress on their ears.

A few more cautious steps and they were in a position to command the point where the track debouched through the last straggle of growth onto the narrow stretch of beach that fringed the river. On the far side of the track the killers were waiting.

Here, as had been prearranged, the posse crouched low, guns ready. The cloud wrack had thinned and the moonlight was fairly bright, revealing large objects plainly. On the south bank of the river a lantern waved back and forth, the signal from the buyers to come ahead, all clear.

Down the track streamed the bitterly complaining cattle, spreading out along the stretch of beach, thrusting thirsty noses into the water.

Pressing on the heels of the last stragglers came the bunched riders. It was easy to see that they were tensely alert, expectant. From the waiting posse came no sound.

One of the riders, Slade noted, was tall and broad and bearded. He wished he could get a better look at the fellow's features, but the pale moonlight was deceptive.

From the brush on the far side of the trail stole four men, holstering their guns in their hands. One called: "Reckon you guessed wrong, boss, nobody showed up. Looks like everything is in the clear." The horsemen relaxed, turning their attention to the cows. Slade nudged the sheriff. Calder straighted a little, his voice rang out,

"Up! In the name of the law! You are under arrest!"

9

A storm of startled exclamations, a clutching of weapons! "Let them have it!" Slade roared, and shot with both hands, his targets the outlaws on the ground. Two fell, writhing and jerking. The posse guns boomed, and a third was down. The one remaining turned to flee, but Estevan's knife hissed through the air and he went down beside his dead companions. Bullets whined over the crouching posse as the mounted wide-loopers opened fire. But their terrified horses were unmanageable, leaping and bucking, and the shots went wild.

However, the cavorting of the horses was to the outlaws' advantage also, as was the uncertain moonlight. Slade steadied his Colts and one saddle was emptied. A voice boomed an order and the owlhoots still in their hulls whirled their mounts and went streaking up the track between the brush, but not soon enough to save still another of their number.

"Hold it!" Slade shouted to the posse, which was blazing away at nothing.

"They're gone, what's left of them," he added. "Hold your guns on those devils on the ground till we make sure of them. Their sort just wounded is as dangerous as a broken-back rattler."

However, examination showed the six downed owlhoots were capable of no more nefarious activities in this world.

"Go up top the slope and see if those two horses stayed around," Slade said. "The other four should be tethered in the brush somewhere. We'll need them to pack the bodies to town. Next chore is to round up the cattle and get them headed home. I see by the burns that they're Dixon Lanham's critters, which I expected they'd be."

The cows had quieted and were cropping the scanty grass that grew at the edge of the growth. Slade decided to allow them to graze for a half-hour or so before getting them in marching order and on their way back to the Square L pastures, no chore for five experienced range riders.

The deputies appeared with the two owl-hoot horses, which had not run far. The other four were found secured to branches in the chaparral. The bodies were loaded and secured in place.

"We'll look them over when we reach the office," Slade said. Calder rubbed his hands together complacently.

"Not a bad night's work," he said. "Saved the cows — better'n a hundred and fifty head I make the count — and did for six sidewinders."

"Not too bad," Slade agreed, "although it could have been better. I'm pretty sure the big, bearded devil is the head of the bunch, and he made it in the clear again."

"You didn't get a good look at him?" the sheriff asked.

"About all I got to see was beard and hat-brim," Slade replied. "That and his build and carriage," he added thoughtfully. "Those things are very hard to disguise."

"You figure the whiskers were false?"

"Very likely," Slade answered. "I'm not prepared to say definitely they were, but I rather think so. Oh, well, perhaps better luck next time. Let's get started, I'm hungry."

"I'm ready to topple over," Calder said. "And I get the shivers when I think of what would have happened if we'd ridden up to that ford. That's just what we would have done if I'd been handling things. You sure figured it right to save our hides for us."

"The set-up was fairly obvious," Slade

deprecated his action. "The head of the bunch would know that if we had caught on that he intended a little chore of cow stealing, the logical thing for us to do was hole up by the ford and wait for the cattle to show. We did just that once before, if you'll remember. So the shrewd horned toad figured to get the jump on us with a little holing-up of his own. I couldn't help but wonder a mite about that and concluded it would be best to give the situation a once-over and not stick our necks out. Appeared I guessed right."

"Uh-huh, and if you hadn't guessed what nobody else did, our necks would have been out, all right, plumb out of commission in this world. Okay, cows, get moving, we've got places to go."

The dawn was breaking in scarlet and rose when they shoved their weary and disgusted charges onto the Square L pastures near the casa. The racket had aroused Lanham and his hands and all were outside, shouting, questioning, when the posse rode into the ranchhouse yard.

An astonished and very grateful man was Dixon Lanham, when the situation was explained. Sheriff Calder did the talking for the posse and gave credit where credit was due. Lanham shook hands with Slade and thanked him profusely, for the loss would have been a heavy one he could have ill afforded.

"Never thought of the hellions runnin' 'em by way of the Circle C holding," he said. "Wasn't patrolling much up to the north. Got sorta careless, I reckon, because old Tim and his boys always took care of that angle — no running anything west over their spread. Forgot things would be different with them pulling out and leaving the holding vacant. Say, the blasted wind spiders didn't waste any time taking advantage."

"For all they knew, Sefton and Boyer might be planning to shove another crew onto the holding without delay and they figured they'd better grasp the opportunity while it existed," Slade explained.

"Guess that's right," agreed Lanham. "Well, come on in to breakfast. The cook's already busy. Feels plumb honored that *El Halcón* will be here for a surrounding. The boys will look after the horses."

"Best thing you've said yet," declared the sheriff.

After a bountiful meal and an hour of relaxation with pipe and cigarette, giving the horses a chance to rest, the posse loaded up and set out for Brownsville, arriving at the river town before noon and creating plenty of excitement as the grisly cortege threaded through the streets to the sheriff's office, where ready volunteers packed in the bodies and laid them out on the floor. Several individuals maintained vaguely that they had seen one or more of the unsavory sextet in town.

Finally the sheriff said, "Come back this evening and look 'em over more closely. Right now we crave a session of ear-pounding."

He shooed out the curious, locked the door. The horses were cared for and everybody went to bed.

It was near nightfall when, after a refreshing sleep, Slade and the sheriff, with the door locked and the window blinds drawn, examined the bodies carefully.

"Ornery-looking specimens," was Calder's verdict. About average border scum, Slade said.

"Less money in their pockets than the last bunch turned out," observed Calder. "I've a notion the setbacks have begun to hurt."

"Very likely," Slade agreed, "and that presages trouble for us. The head of the outfit must do something fast to bolster morale and provide his horned toads with spending money such as they have become

113

accustomed to of late."

"Which means the hellions will try to pull something soon, eh?" the sheriff growled.

"Definitely," Slade said. "Our chore is to endeavor to anticipate what they have in mind, and if possible do something to circumvent it."

"You did a sorta good job of anticipatin' last night," Calder pointed out. "A few more like that and we'll be settin' pretty."

"Last night everything was so obvious," Slade smiled. The sheriff snorted derisively.

"Uh-huh, as I've said before, so obvious that everybody else plumb overlooked it." Slade laughed, and for moments sat gazing out the window at the red glory of the sunset. Calder watched him expectantly.

"Now what's cookin' in your think tank?" he finally asked. "I know that look."

"I was just thinking," Slade replied, "that it is sometimes possible to put two and two together and make five."

"Whatever that means," sighed the sheriff. "This much I gather, that you're getting a sorta notion as to who is the head of the owlhoot bunch. Right?"

"Possibly, if the mathematical absurdity turns out to be sound," Slade answered smilingly.

"And only the devil himself knows what

114

in blazes that means," retorted Calder. "Say, I've had no breakfast, and I reckon you haven't either, so let's mosey to the Blue Bell for a surrounding before half the town wants in to take a look at the carcasses and Doc Cooper shows up to hold an inquest."

"To quote one of your favorite remarks, that's the best thing you've said yet," Slade chuckled, rising to his feet. The sheriff grinned.

When they reached the Blue Bell, Boyer at once joined them.

"So, I understand you caught some wide-loopers trespassing on my property, Mr. Slade," he chuckled. "Fine! Well, the deal is closed, I banked Sefton's money, drew a check for Ester and told him goodbye this afternoon. Thanks for looking over the papers, Mr. Slade. Tim's headed west and Sefton and I are now co-owners of the Circle C holding."

"Anybody else make Tim Ester an offer for the property?" Slade asked casually. Boyer shook his head.

"Nobody else appeared interested," he replied. Slade nodded and changed the topic of conversation. Calder shot him a sharp look but did not comment.

"I'm heading for the kitchen to make sure you get a proper celebration surrounding,"

Boyer announced. "And I'll make folks leave you alone until you've finished eating. Got a notion you're hungry."

"My stomach thinks my throat's sewed up," declared Calder. "Tell the cook to do his darndest." Boyer laughed and betook himself to the kitchen.

The two law enforcement officers enjoyed a leisurely meal topped off with a final cup of coffee and a cigarette for Slade, a snort and his pipe for the sheriff. He nodded to Boyer and the owner allowed the congratulatory citizens to descend on Slade.

El Halcón endured their plaudits until Boyer took pity on him and appeared with a handful of papers he said he wished Slade to examine. The crowd drifted away and soon were occupied with the drinks, the cards, and the girls.

"Well, guess we'd better toddle back to the office," the sheriff said. "Folks will want to look the carcasses over, and the coroner will show up to hold his darn fool inquest in another hour or so."

Again quite a few persons were confident they had seen the outlaws, or some of them, in town, and that was all. Doc Cooper interrupted speculations by appearing with his coroner's jury.

The inquest was fairly brief, Slade, Calder

and the two deputies testifying. Estevan was not present. Calder once more cleared the office and locked the door. The undertaker would arrive shortly to take charge of the bodies.

"Two used to be cowhands, the others never were," Slade replied to the sheriff's question.

"And what the devil were they?" Calder wondered. Slade shrugged.

"River or Gulf pirates, perhaps, or maybe smugglers," he said. "Doesn't really matter. They were apprehended violating Texas law."

"And they won't do it again," the sheriff observed cheerfully, "and that's what really counts. Now what?"

"Now across the river to the cantina to see if Amado or Estevan has something to tell us," Slade decided. "I think we can depend on nothing happening tonight. But you never can tell for sure."

"Not with the sidewinders we're up against," Calder agreed. "Okay, let's go."

They took their time crossing the bridge, and were watchful, although Slade did not really anticipate trouble.

Without incident, they reached the cantina, to find it plenty busy, with the evening still early. Calder continued with Amado to their reserved table, but Slade paused to chat with Estevan, who was lounging at the near end of the bar.

After a few minutes of general conversation, he gave the knife man some surprising instructions. At least they would have seemed surprising to the average individual. But nothing ever surprised Estevan. He merely bowed, and said, "Of a certainty, *Capitán,* it shall be done." He finished his drink and sauntered out.

Slade joined Amado and the sheriff. Dolores came over from the floor and flopped down beside him, snuggling her hand in his.

"Plenty of business, but nice and peaceful, so far," she said. "Sure hope it stays that way the rest of the night."

"I've a notion it will," Slade replied. "After last night, there should be a lull in various activities."

"You're darn right," said Calder. "I figure the hellions are busy licking their wounds. But I don't know, that sort doesn't bruise easy and recovers darn fast."

"Don't be pessimistic," Dolores chided. "Look on the bright side."

"Uh-huh, they say every cloud has a silver lining," grunted the sheriff. "Could be, but the side turned toward us down here can be darn dark." Dolores trilled laughter and

118

jumped to her feet.

"Come on, Walt, let's dance," she said. "Leave this prophet of gloom to his dire forebodings."

"In his glass is distilled sunshine," quoted Amado. "Soon he with good cheer will be filled. Waiter!"

10

The night jogged along. La Luz was gay, hilarious, but with no trouble developing, so far. Dolores went on the floor for a while. Amado repaired to his post at the far end of the bar, next to the till. Slade and the sheriff relaxed in comfort.

"Hello!" the latter exclaimed, "here comes Vibart Sefton."

The lawyer waved to Calder, nodded to Slade, and joined Amado at the bar.

"Feller looks tired," Calder commented. "Looks like he's been doing some riding, too; clothes all dusty. May have been looking over his new holding. Yes?"

"Possibly," Slade conceded.

A few minutes passed and Estevan strolled in. He nodded slightly to Slade, accepted the drink the bartender poured, and bowed to *El Halcón*. Slade regarded Sefton, his eyes thoughtful, which the sheriff did not fail to notice. However, he made no remark and puffed stolidly on his pipe. Slade rolled a cigarette and ordered more coffee.

"Hmmm!" said Calder. " 'Pears to be old-home-week for new settlers in the section. Here's Mostyn Selby, the Albemarle owner. Looks like he's been doing some riding, too."

Selby glanced around, waved a greeting and proceeded to the end of the bar. He nodded to Sefton and engaged Amado in conversation.

"Believe I mentioned to you that he was interested in tying onto a place this side of the river," said the sheriff. "Expect he's discussing it with Amado again."

"It is possible," Slade said. "Yes, I recall you said he would like to establish here."

"And you said it would be a good notion," Calder reminded.

"Matamoros is up and coming, no doubt as to that," was Slade's reply. The sheriff's brows knitted, but he did not comment.

Selby didn't stay long. He finished his drink and sauntered out, pausing long enough to call out, "Keep the good work going, Mr. Slade. A little more and this will be a decent section for honest people."

"Thank you, Mr. Selby," the Ranger acknowledged. "I hope you are right."

"Yep, a rather nice sort," observed the sheriff.

Sefton came over to the table. "Wanted to thank you for looking over the papers dealing with our purchase of the Circle C, Mr. Slade," he said. "Boyer sets plenty of store by your judgment, and I figure he is right. Be seeing you; feel like prowling around a bit and having a powwow with some of the boys." He swaggered to the door, his big shoulders swinging.

Calder watched him go, and muttered something under his mustache. A few moments later, Estevan glided to the kitchen. Still another moment and Slade saw the glass upper panel of the kitchen door go blank. That, he knew, was the lamp being turned down while Estevan slipped out the back door into a dark alley. A second or two and light again glowed through the panel. Perhaps five minutes elapsed and the procedure was repeated. Then the kitchen door opened a crack to reveal the cook. Immediately it closed. Slade stood up.

"Come on," he said, "Estevan has hit on something."

They made their leisurely way to the kitchen, closing the door after them.

Estevan wasted no time. "Men three by the corner stand, hands on guns, watching

122

the cantina door," he said. "Doubtless they await *Capitán* to out that door go. We out the back door will go. The light turn out again, Enrique," he said to the cook. "Only to my knock open."

The light went out. Another instant and all three were in the dark alley that paralleled the street the cantina building fronted on.

Slowly, cautiously, they stole along toward the corner, a little distance away, hugging the building wall, where the shadows were deepest.

They spotted the three drygulchers, also in the shadow, staring toward the cantina's swinging doors. A few more slow steps, and Slade called softly:

"Good evening, gentlemen!"

Startled exclamations! The trio whirled toward the sound of his voice, going for their holsters.

Slade drew and shot with both hands. Estevan's knife buzzed through the air. The sheriff's gun boomed thrice. Peering through the powder fog, Slade saw that all three killers were sprawled motionless on the ground.

Estevan dashed forward and retrieved his blade, shaking the ruddy drops from the gleaming steel. He and his companions sped back to the kitchen door, which opened at Estevan's double tap. They glided in and the cook turned up the lamp.

The cantina was pandemonium redoubled. Shouts, curses in three languages, a banging of overturned tables and chairs, the beat of feet toward the swinging doors, the shrieks of dance floor girls blended in an uproar that quivered the roof beams.

Slade led the way from the kitchen, and slammed into Dolores, a gun in her hand.

"Quick, back to our table," Slade told her. She obeyed without hesitating. They were seated when men began running back in, bellowing, gesturing. A young cowhand dashed to the table.

"Sh-sheriff," he chattered, "Sheriff, there's three dead men in the street by the corner of the alley!"

"That so?" Calder replied composedly. The informant appeared somewhat taken aback at the reception of what he considered startling news.

"I — I —" he began.

"It is no concern of ours," Slade told him. "We are Texas peace officers. This is Mexico, where we have no authority. The *jefe politico* — the Matamoros Chief of Police — will take care of the matter."

"Reckon that's so, never thought of it,"

said the subdued cowhand.

However, the rest of the cantina was far from subdued. The uproar continued, with wild conjectures flying about. Nobody appeared to know the deceased, or if they did, refrained from admitting it. Who killed them quickly became the basis of fierce arguments, although the consensus veered to the contention that they had some sort of a falling out and gunned each other.

"Chances are that will be the chief's conclusion," Slade remarked as the cowhand headed for the bar. "He'll know very well who are the responsible parties but will refrain from saying so, to keep us out of it. He'll be showing here before long. How you feel, Dolores?"

"I've got the shakes," the girl replied. "Pardon me for what I said a little while ago, Uncle Tom; you are without doubt a prophet of honor in your own land." The sheriff chuckled and sampled his glass.

"Suppose you tell me just what did go on out there," Dolores suggested.

Calder obliged, in detail, the girl listening intently, sighing resignedly when he finished and gazing at Slade.

"The way he tells it, you'd imagine I was playing a lone hand," Slade said smilingly.

"As it happened, he and Estevan were there, too."

"Why did those awful men think you were coming out soon?" wondered Dolores.

"Somebody has very sharp ears," Slade replied obliquely.

"Sharp ears?"

"That's right. Just a little while before, as he moved to the bar for a few minutes, I told Tom I thought I'd stroll around a bit for a change. I don't think I raised my voice, but somebody heard, and set the neat little trap that Estevan kept from being sprung, decidedly to my advantage."

The sheriff looked startled, but said nothing. Dolores shook her curly head.

"I'm going on the floor for a while longer," she said. "Please keep out of trouble this time until I return. We've had enough excitement for one night." She kissed Slade's cheek and trotted to the dance floor.

"Hmmm!" the sheriff remarked. "Vibart Sefton went out right after you mentioned to me that you figured to take a walk."

"Tighten the latigo," Slade cautioned. "So did Chris Preston, the manager of the Cascade warehouse, and Mostyn Selby, the Albemarle saloon owner."

"Okay! Okay!" snorted Calder. "I'll button my lip. The old police chief should be here any minute now. Will be interesting to hear what he'll have to say."

For a while the killings were the subject of animated discussion, but not for too long. Violent death was too commonplace to the Border country to make any very lasting impression. Except perhaps on those who suffered untimely decease, a moot question.

The old *jefe politico* strolled in, accepted a chair and a glass of wine.

"Hombres from north of the river," he said, without preamble. "The world of the living has naught lost."

He glanced suggestively at Slade, who recounted the gunfight in the alley mouth, and what led up to it. The chief nodded his wise old head.

"So! *El Halcón,* the good, the just, they would kill. But in the hand of *El Halcón* is death. And *El Dios,* who treasures the good, ever guards him."

"Thank you, Chief," Slade said soberly.

"Would *Capitán* like the remains to view?" the chief asked, draining his glass. "In my office are they."

"Yes, I would," Slade replied. "Let's go."

They walked out, with eyes following their progress to the swinging doors, including the worried big and blue ones of Dolores. Slade waved to her, and smiled reassuringly.

The dead outlaws, hard-looking specimens, were laid out on the floor, awaiting the undertaker. Slade examined them closely, especially their hands.

"Were never cowhands," he announced.

"Scourings from the Devil's kettle," said the chief. Sheriff Calder growled assent.

"Of money there was in their pockets some," explained the chief. "Enough to them bury. What else was in the pockets is on the table, there; does *Capitán* it care to examine."

There was nothing of interest in the collection of junk, so far as Slade could see, until he came to a folded paper that appeared to have been torn from a pad. On it was a row of figures, added, and across the face was written in a neat and clerkly hand the single word, "Roof." Slade gazed at it, the concentration furrow between his black brows deepening, a sign *El Halcón* was doing some thinking.

"What the devil is it?" Calder asked.

"Appears to be a bill from a saloon for drinks, doubtless presented by a bartender," Slade replied slowly. " 'Roof' is in different handwriting, bar owner's slang for 'On the house.' Would appear the gentleman's credit was very good somewhere."

"Where?" wondered the sheriff.

"That," Slade answered, "I would very much like to know."

"Why?"

"Because it would definitely identify someone with whom he had been associated on very good terms."

"Verily the eye of *El Halcón* sees all!" murmured the chief.

The sheriff tugged his mustache, looked puzzled and thoughtful.

Saying goodnight to the chief, they returned to the cantina, to find the crowd pretty well thinned out, Amado sounding his last call. Dolores had changed to a street dress, the girls had left the floor. Everybody called it a night.

11

The following afternoon, Sheriff Calder regarded the floor of his office with disapproval.

"Just don't look right with nothing on it," he complained.

"Wouldn't be surprised if we soon have an opportunity to remedy that," Slade said. "I think we can look forward to some hectic activity in the next few days."

"Figure the hellions will try to pull something, eh?"

"Little doubt about it, I'd say," Slade replied.

A tap on the door sounded. Calder opened it to admit a messenger from the telegraph office.

"Telegram for Mr. Slade," he said.

Slade unfolded the sheet, and read:

"Brownsville Thursday
(signed) Dunn"

Without comment, he passed it to Calder.

"So!" the sheriff chuckled as he perused the terse missive from General Manager James G. "Jaggers" Dunn of the great C. & P. Railroad System. "So the old Empire Builder hankers for some advice from the best engineer that ever rode across Texas!"

"I fear you and Mr. Dunn are both prone to exaggerate," Slade smiled.

"Nope," the sheriff said conclusively.

Neither the sheriff nor General Manager Dunn was too far wrong. Shortly before the death of his father after financial reverses that entailed the loss of the elder Slade's ranch, young Walt had graduated with high honors from a famous college of engineering. He had planned to take a post-graduate course in certain subjects to round out his education and better fit him for the profession he had hoped to make his life's work.

That, however, became impossible for the time being and he was to a certain extent at loose ends and couldn't decide just which way to turn. So when Captain Jim McNelty, with whom he had worked some during summer vacations, suggested that he sign up with the Rangers for a while and continue his studies in his spare time, Slade thought the idea a good one.

So Walt Slade became a Texas Ranger.

Long since, he had gotten more from private study than he could have hoped for from post-graduate study and was eminently fitted for the profession of engineering. He had received offers of lucrative employment from such outstanding figures of the business and financial world as Jaggers Dunn, former Texas Governor, oil millionaire Jim Hogg, and John Warne "Bet-a-Million" Gates, the Wall Street tycoon.

But meanwhile Ranger work had gotten a strong hold on him, providing as it did so many opportunities for helping the deserving, suppressing evil, promoting good, and making the wonderful land he loved a still better land for the right kind of people.

So, as he had told himself a number of times, until the repetition was beginning to become a bit dubious, he was young; plenty of time to be an engineer. He would stick with the Rangers for a while longer.

Slade turned Jaggers Dunn's message over in his slim fingers, gazing at it abstractly, the concentration furrow deepening between his black brows.

"Thursday," he remarked musingly. "Today is Tuesday. The Old Man should be here day after tomorrow. Wonder just what *is* on his mind. Will be something interesting, I wager."

"It always is," said the sheriff. "And you have no notion as to what he has on his mind?"

"Yes, I believe I have," Slade replied slowly. "I believe that, for one thing, he will want to look over the Circle C holding and if he finds it suitable for his project, which I am sure he will, I think he will make a deal with Boyer and Sefton and then announce his intention of building the line south to link with the Mexican road."

"And that," said Calder, "will stir up a flurry here, for it will sure boost business. Do *you* consider the Circle C land suitable to his project?"

"I do," Slade answered.

"Then everything is all settled," the sheriff declared cheerfully. "Yep, all settled."

Slade laughed, and didn't argue the point.

"And now," said Calder, "suppose we celebrate the coming prosperity with a surrounding and a few snorts at the Blue Bell. Reckon Dolores went to work early, didn't she?"

"Wouldn't be surprised if she did," Slade replied smilingly.

"And I ain't had no breakfast either," said the sheriff with a chuckle. "Let's go!"

They found the Blue Bell quite busy, even though the hour was still early. Calder

133

chuckled again after they gave their order.

"Guess Boyer is going to be a flabbergasted gent when he hears the news," he said. "And he'll give you the credit for everything."

"An undeserved credit, I'd say," Slade replied.

"Oh, I reckon not," disagreed the sheriff. "If you don't okay the land for Dunn, he wouldn't buy it. Now would he?"

"Mr. Dunn usually makes his own decisions," Slade equivocated.

"Me, I can't keep from thinking about that darn slip of paper with 'Roof' written across it you found in the dead owlhoot's pocket," Calder added.

"I'm thinking about it, too," Slade said grimly. "For it may be the little slip that will turn out to be a big one."

"Yes?"

"Yes. Because, in my opinion it definitely shows that the head of the outlaw bunch is a saloonowner."

The sheriff looked decidedly startled. "Wouldn't be surprised," he said. "Most rumhole owners fit into the picture, all right." He regarded his glass, cocked an eye at the ceiling.

"Got any notion who might be the gent who did that writing?" he asked with elaborated casualness.

"Yes, I have," Slade answered. "We'll discuss it later. Right now let's forget all about the matter and eat."

Which they proceeded to do.

Finally, full-fed and content, they relaxed with pipe and cigarette and for a while smoked in silence. After a while, the sheriff spoke.

"And you really figure to know who is the gent who sets 'em up for owlhoots," he remarked.

"Yes," Slade said slowly. "Yes, the man who was always in evidence just before an attempt against my life was made. The tall, broad-shouldered man who escaped with the money from the burned Cascade warehouse. The man who, looking over the ground in anticipation of a little chore of widelooping, rode down the Circle C holding and set a very shrewd drygulching try for me that came very near succeeding. The man who managed to escape the night the Port Isabel train was wrecked. And who set that very neat trap for us the night Dixon Lanham's cows were rustled, and who, his luck continuing to hold good, escaped again, leaving half a dozen of his followers dead in the dust. Beginning to understand?"

"The feller you saw riding the Circle C

spread down from the north! For the love of Pete, you don't mean —"

The sheriff's voice trailed off incredulously and he stared wide-eyed at *El Halcón*.

"Yes," Slade replied composedly, "that's just whom I mean — *Mostyn Selby!*"

"And I said something a little while ago about Fats Boyer going to be flabbergasted!" groaned Calder. "Well, he's sure got company; the last hellion I'd have thought of."

"Oh, he's a smart one, all right," Slade said. "But like all the brand, he made a few little slips that, to employ a hackneyed expression, put the finger on him."

"And I been looking sorta sideways at Vibart Sefton," the sheriff sighed. Slade laughed.

"Just a big woolly bear, Dolores would describe him," he said. "Sets up to be mean and hard, out only for himself. Can be plenty tough physically if necessary, but really, inside he's soft as butter. I discussed him with Amado and learned how he got justice for quite a few poor folks and refused to take a penny for his services. That's why I was so pleased when I learned about the deal for the Circle C spread he and Boyer were making. The poor devil will, most unexpectedly, tie onto a nice fat sum of *dinero,* which he can use, if we can talk him into hanging on to most of it. He's as bad as Boyer when it comes to giving away money. But I've a notion they both sleep well."

"And," said Calder, "if pressed, I could name somebody else who don't suffer from insomnia."

"Thank you, Tom," Slade replied. "I do the best I can."

"Which is plenty much," declared the sheriff. "But the question right now is what are we going to do about that blankety-blank killer 'fore he murders somebody else."

"Frankly, I don't know," Slade answered. "But Estevan and his *amigos* are trailing him and watching his every move. They may soon have something to tell us."

"Hope so," growled Calder. "I'm itchin' for a chance to line sights with that sidewinder. Suppose we'll be ambling over to the cantina after a bit?"

"Yes, I think it will be a good notion," Slade agreed. "This is a *fiesta* day in Mata-moros and things will be lively, with pos-sibly something that will give us a break. Somehow I have a hunch there will be."

"You and your hunches!" snorted the sheriff. "But blast it, they're almost always straight. Have some more, real fast!"

Slade laughed, then exclaimed in low tones. "Watch your expression! And keep your voice down, I think he has very sharp ears."

The reason for his caution was the entrance of the man they had been discussing, Mostyn Selby himself.

Selby glanced around, waved a greeting, which the sheriff managed to return, although Slade felt it strained the old peace officer's digestive tract to do so. Selby sauntered to the far end of the bar and engaged Boyer in conversation.

"You figure the hellion don't know we suspect him?" Calder muttered.

"That's my opinion, and it is to our advantage to keep him that way as long as possible," Slade returned. "Then there's always the chance he'll grow careless, and perhaps make the real slip we're hoping for. If he comes over, be nice to him."

"I'll end up clawing the rafters," the sheriff growled. "Hope he doesn't stay long; raises my blood pressure just to look at him."

"You'll manage to survive," Slade said smilingly. "It isn't the first time you've been called upon to put on such an act; you always managed to get by."

"Uh-huh, but I can't help but feel the horned toad is laughing at us," replied

Calder. "He'll laugh on the other side of his face before you're finished with him. And all I hanker for is just one good whack at him."

"Chances are you'll get it," Slade predicted cheerfully.

Selby had a couple of drinks and departed, smiling and nodding as he passed the table.

"Wouldn't be surprised if the devil came in here to keep tabs on you," snorted the sheriff.

"Could be," Slade conceded. "But Estevan and his boys are keeping tabs on him, so it doesn't matter. Well, how about moseying across the river?"

"Suits me," replied Calder.

They waved to Boyer and walked out into the scarlet and gold glory of the sunset.

"Say!" the sheriff suddenly exclaimed, "just came to think of it — Selby's rumhole, the Albemarle, was robbed, shortly before you showed up this time. Does that mean another bunch is operating in the section?"

Slade smiled and shook his head. "Nope, that was just an example of Selby's cunning," he explained. "Hardly anybody would think he'd rob himself, but that's what he did, to throw suspicion away from himself. And, incidentally, to collect insurance on his supposed-to-be loss. Oh, he's a shrewd one, all right, perhaps just a little too shrewd for his own good. Well, we'll see."

12

Reaching Matamoros, they found the streets thronged with *fiesta* celebrants dressed in charro costumes, gay with color, including silver-encrusted sombreros, red, yellow and blue embroidered serapes and velvet pantaloons. The air vibrated to the strumming of guitars by wandering troubadours who gathered at street corners to sing the folk songs of old Mexico.

Slade slowed the pace as they made their way to the cantina, for he always found the scene interesting.

They found the cantina also crowded, lively and gay. Dolores waved from the dance floor, Amado from the far end of the bar. Estevan was not in evidence at the moment. Slade felt that very likely he was keeping tabs on Mostyn Selby in person.

The sheriff ordered a snort, Slade coffee. A waiter came from the back room bearing a bottle of Amado's favorite golden wine.

Slade accepted a glass to go with his coffee.

"Makes a good chaser for redeye," said Calder as he filled a crystal goblet to the brim. He glanced around the crowded room.

"By gosh, she is booming tonight," he said. "Can't say that I've ever seen the darn rumhole so filled up."

"It is Matamoros' most important *fiesta,*" Slade replied. "Celebrates the founding of the town, which in reality is not much older than Brownsville but has been battered and battle-scarred into a semblance of antiquity. It has been burned twice, and pillaged more than once. Yes, it's going to be a booming night. Perhaps we, too, will be able to do some business — never can tell. Perhaps Estevan will have something on tap when he shows up."

"He's busy, all right, you can depend on that," nodded Calder. "Here comes your gal; sure looks cute tonight, skirt even shorter than usual."

Dolores was bright-eyed and rosy, her piquant face animated as she sat down close to Slade.

"Phe-e-ew!" she exclaimed, "I'm out of breath already, and the night has just started. Just the same, you're going to dance with me or I'll know the reason why. And that isn't all."

"Hmmm!" observed the sheriff. "*That* sounds interesting."

Dolores made a face at him, and refrained from vocal comment. She had a glass of wine and flounced back to the floor, flashing Slade a smile over her shoulder.

A few minutes later, Estevan glided in. Slade caught his eye and beckoned. Estevan approached the table, accepted a chair and a glass of wine. He glanced inquiringly at the sheriff. Slade nodded.

"The *ladrone,* Selby, his cantina left with five others," Estevan said. "They mounted *caballos* hitched at the rack and rode north to the trail. There they turned west. I thought it not wise to follow farther."

"Very wise," Slade interpolated. Estevan nodded agreement.

"Did they ride furtively by way of dark streets?" Slade asked. Estevan shook his head.

"Quite openly they rode," he replied, "even to speaking to certain ones on the street the *ladrone* seemed to know."

"Nothing unusual about that," put in the sheriff. "Rumhole owners know everybody. And you have no notion where they were headed for?" Again the knife man shook his head; Estevan was not one to waste words.

The sheriff turned to Slade.

"Going to follow the devils?" he asked.

"Would be just a waste of time," *El Halcón* replied. "No notion where they are headed for or what's in their minds. Besides, they have a head start and can turn off any-where."

"Where *could* the hellions be headed for?"

"In my opinion, Brownsville," Slade said. The sheriff's eyes widened.

"Now what the devil do you mean by that?" he demanded.

"I mean that after they've ridden far enough to be sure nobody is keeping tabs on them, they'll circle back to town, where they plan to pull something, on that I'll wager. What? Your guess is good as mine."

"We the streets watch, do the *ladrones* return, know will we, and will *Capitán* tell," put in Estevan.

"And that may provide us with an op-portunity to frustrate the devils," Slade said. "Anyhow, we have plenty of time. They will hardly return before midnight. So take it easy."

"And you're going to find out mighty soon what Dolores meant when she said dance with her isn't all you're going to do," chuckled the sheriff. "See? She and the orchestra leader are having a palaver, and he just picked up his guitar."

The leader had indeed seized the instrument, which he began waving. He bowed in Slade's direction and he stepped to the edge of the little raised platform that accommodated the musicians. His voice rang out —

"*Señoritas* and *Señores!* Quiet, please! *Capitán* will sing!"

The sheriff chuckled again, and twinkled his eyes at Slade.

"Well, guess it wouldn't be nice to make the gent a liar," Slade said, rising to his feet.

"*El Halcón! El Halcón!*" shouted voices as he made his way to the platform and accepted the guitar. Then a hush of expectancy fell over the room. Slade flashed the white smile of *El Halcón,* and sang.

Music, the universal language, is a dream translated into sound, the expression of a mood, a thought. The truly great artist realizes and understands that truth and endeavors to reach his hearers by striking chords of mood within them.

So for the dock workers and the rivermen he sang of the tawny flood of the Rio Grande and the blue Gulf with which it merged its waters. For the cowhands and *vaqueros* present he sang of the green and golden rangeland, its beauties and its terror.

145

For the railroaders the song of the clanking siderods, the booming exhaust and the grinding wheels that played so large a part in the winning of the West.

And as his great golden baritone-bass pealed and thundered through the room, each listener saw his own dreams pass in review, and through the magic of that voice saw, at least dimly, their dreams' consummation. Sufficient unto Eternity is the glory of the Hour!

Turning to the dance floor, he concluded with a dreamy love song of old *Mejico,* poignant with winsome appeal.

Through thunders of applause that shook the rafters, he made his way back to the table and the girl who waited there, her blue eyes misty.

"The singingest man in the whole Southwest," said the sheriff.

"And with the gunhand the fastest is," added Estevan.

Right on both counts!

The hours jogged along. Slade and Dolores had their dances together, although the floor was so crowded there was barely room to shuffle. That, however, made for holding partners closer, so nobody complained.

Finally Slade glanced at the clock. "Guess

we'd better be moving," he said. "Across to the Blue Bell and await developments."

Waving to Amado and Dolores, they departed, anxious eyes following them to the door. Slowly, they wormed their way through the crowded streets to the bridge-head; ascending the ramp, they crossed, watchful and alert, although Slade did not really anticipate trouble. He reasoned that Selby had all or nearly all of his followers with him. However, with such a character it was best not to take chances.

Brownsville was quieter than Matamoros, the streets not at all crowded. They reached the Blue Bell without incident and occupied the table Boyer reserved for them. Estevan had a glass of wine and then glided out to keep in touch with his *amigos,* who were watching the streets leading from the north and west.

With a snort, coffee and cigarettes, they relaxed comfortably and bided their time. It was now very close to midnight.

"Those young fellers are sure all right," the sheriff remarked, speaking of Estevan and his boys.

"Yes, they don't come any better," Slade agreed. "As loyal friends, Yaqui-Mexicans are hard to beat. Capable, too, in every sense of the word. I've had dealings with them at Laredo, El Paso, and elsewhere, and they're always the same. With you till the last brand is run."

A half hour or so passed and it was a little past midnight, and Estevan returned, his black eyes snapping, his hand caressing the haft of his throwing knife. He came straight to the table and said, without preamble:

"The *ladrones* returned, by way of the dark and lonely streets the railroad by. On Twelfth Street they turned east and to the corner of Washington rode, where stands a large grove. Into the grove they rode and did not at once reappear, doubtless because on the street some people moving about were, not many. That was but the minute few agone. To inform *Capitán* I hastened."

"Twelfth and Washington Streets," repeated the sheriff. "What the blazes? Nothing there."

"Just a minute," Slade said. "Tom, there is something there, the Market House — it runs on Twelfth from Washington to Adams Street, the full block."

"But heck, there's never any money in that blasted market," the sheriff protested. "I happen to know they bank every day."

"That's right," Slade conceded, "but remember, the City Hall is on the second floor of that building, over toward Washington Street, and I feel safe in saying that every now and then there's more than a little in the office safe there."

"By gosh, that's so," agreed Calder. "Quite a passel at times, and, like all politicians, they're sorta careless about it. I've seen the safe standing wide open, though I reckon they lock it at night. You figure the hellions might be making a try for it?"

"Stranger things have happened," Slade replied. "Let's see, now, the grove Estevan mentioned is on both sides of Twelfth Street — street cuts right through it. Did you notice on which side of the street they entered the grove, Estevan?"

"The side west," the knife man instantly responded.

"Okay, we'll slide down Jefferson Street to Eleventh Street, cut over west and enter the grove from the north and work our way down to Twelfth Street close to Washington Street until we can get a view of the Market Building and see what we can figure."

Without delay they left the Blue Bell and executed the maneuver successfully. They paused in the shadow of the trees and surveyed the building. It was dark save for one window that, Slade knew, opened into the first of the three office rooms occupied by City Hall. A dim light glowed back of that window.

"I'm willing to bet they are in there opening the safe," Slade whispered. "The question is, how are we going to get in without getting blown from under our hats. There's only one stairway to the second floor, and it leads down to a door opening right on the street, and we sure can't use that door. From the offices a long hall runs the length of the building, clear to Adams Street. Somewhere over there is our only chance to enter the building without being seen. Let's go, keep in the shadow, and keep quiet."

In utter silence they glided along close to the building, and they had nearly reached the Adams Street end of the building when Slade halted.

Close to the building grew a large tree with a slightly sloping trunk, and right under an open window ran a massive branch that scraped the building wall.

"There's our way in, if we can make it without kicking up a racket," Slade breathed. "Willing to risk it, Tom?"

"I'm willing to risk anything," replied the sheriff in as near a growl as a whisper could achieve. Slade suppressed a chuckle, and tackled the tree. Next came the sheriff, then Estevan, who moved with the silence of a night hawk without the faint rustle of the hawk's wings.

In a matter of minutes, Slade had swung his feet through the window and to the floor. And the instant he was inside the hall, his amazingly keen ears caught a sound drifting from the front of the building, as if a rat with metallic teeth were gnawing a pipe under the floor boards, which he recognized as the soft whine of a drill biting into iron. He reached a warning hand to the sheriff who in another moment was beside him with Estevan close beind.

"They're working on the safe, drilling out the combination knob," Slade breathed. "The odds are against us, but with the element of surprise on our side, I think we should make out. I'm confident they don't suspect a thing, for they are talking together unconcernedly. The safe is in the second office from the front. You must give them a chance to surrender, Tom, then shoot fast and straight. Crouch down low. Let's go!"

Together they eased along the narrow hall, reached the first office, inched across it to the door leading to the dimly lit room. Another moment and Slade halted, almost to the door, from where they had a clear view of the second office.

Crouching in front of the massive old iron safe, a man was skillfully operating a hand drill. Already there were several overlapping holes around the combination knob. Another minute or two and the knob would be lifted out, the safe door opened. Beside the driller stood a tall, bearded man who held a low-turned lamp.

Slade was about to nudge the sheriff, then he abruptly desisted. There were but four men in the office, and Estevan had seen six ride west. Where the devil were the other two?

For moments he stood listening and peering. Gradually he became confident there was nobody in the outer office. Well, whatever the loco set-up was, they had to take a chance; he nudged the sheriff.

"Up!" bawled Calder. "You are under arrest!"

Instantly, the tall, bearded man crashed the lamp to the floor. Darkness swooped down like a thrown blanket, through which blazed orange flashes. Slugs whizzed over the heads of the crouching posse.

A gasping scream sliced through the powder fog as Slade shot with both hands. The hiss of Estevan's knife was echoed by a gurgling shriek. The sheriff's gun boomed, and a third cry echoed the report.

There was a beat of feet on the floor, thudding across the outer office and down the stairs. Slade poured lead in the general direction of the sound, with little hope of scoring a hit. The smoke rings swirled in a draft of cool air as a door banged open.

Slade seized the sheriff's shoulder as he started in pursuit and hauled him back.

"Don't follow!" he snapped. "The other two may have a trap set for us beside the outer door. Quiet, now."

Listening intently, he quickly became convinced the three outlaws on the floor were dead; otherwise he would have heard their breathing. Resolving to take a chance, he whipped across the offices and down the stairs with a quick, lithe tread. But even as he reached the foot of the stairs and the open outer door, there was a muffled beat of horses' irons, fading into the west. And shouting sounded nearby. People who lived not far from the Market Building had been aroused by the shooting and were coming to investigate. Slade turned back from the door.

"Get a light going, Tom," he called. "They're gone."

A lamp flared as he ascended the stairs. Reaching the second office he found Estevan staring at the faces of the three dead outlaws.

"Capitán," the knife man said, "these were

153

not of the five who with the *ladrone* rode west. These I have never seen before."

"And what the devil does that mean?" demanded the sheriff.

"It means that the sidewinder, with his usual cunning, provided an alibi for himself by riding out of town with plenty of people noting the fact," Slade explained. "Then he picked up three more of his bunch to handle the chore here at the Market, with him, wearing his false beard, directing their activities. See where we stand? Still not a thing against *amigo* Selby."

"Well, anyhow we gave three more of the skunks their comeuppance and saved the money in the safe, which the chances are is plenty," the sheriff observed philosophically. He glanced inquiringly at Slade as voices chattered at the foot of the stairs. The Ranger nodded.

"All right, come up and look things over," he called.

Heads poked in, cautiously, volleying questions, which the sheriff answered, giving credit where it was due. Slade was favored with praise he would rather have done without. He created a diversion by requesting that the Market manager or somebody who could take charge of things be notified. Several individuals hurried out

154

to take care of the matter. And to incidentally spread the word far and wide of the happening — with the result that the offices were soon jam-packed with the curious.

The Market manager was first to appear; closely following him, a City Hall official.

"Yes, there's plenty in that safe," he replied to a question from Slade. "You fellers sure did the town a good turn. It won't be forgotten. Yes, I'll look after things here. And some more of the boys will be showing up soon."

"And have these carcasses packed to my office," said the sheriff.

That chore was also quickly cared for, providing Slade an excuse to escape his well-wishers, who were increasing in number by the minute.

Arriving at the office, the bearers placed their burdens on the floor and hurried back to the Market.

"Lock the door, give the bodies a quick once-over, and let's hightail across the river before the crowd begins showing up here," Slade said. Having done that, they headed for the bridge, Estevan having already sped to the cantina with the word that everything was under control, nobody injured.

"That little trick of hunkerin' down low served us good again," observed Calder.

155

"Slugs went over us. Better over than through."

"The devils were caught completely off balance," Slade said. "And were it not for Selby's hair-trigger thinking, we might well have bagged the whole bunch. Out went the light, and he was headed for the stairs, taking advantage of his opportunity to escape. I'd be willing to wager he never fired a shot. Getting in the clear was his whole objective, and he made it.

"But his time will come, no doubt about that," said Calder.

Without interruption, they reached the bridge and crossed it. The *fiesta* was still going strong, and it was doubtful if Matamoros had heard about the robbery attempt. At the cantina, they found Estevan's assurance that all was well, nobody hurt, had smoothed out the various cases of jitters and everybody was gay and happy.

"Might as well pull in your boys, nothing more they can do tonight," Slade told him. "Let them take part in the fun."

"And here's something I took from those three devils' pockets," said the sheriff, shoving a wad of bills into his hand. Guess your *amigos* have earned a little celebration."

Estevan grinned delightedly and hurried out.

Dolores trotted over from the floor. "And I suppose you're both starved," she said.

"Haven't had a bite since breakfast, and that was quite a while ago," Slade admitted.

"And I'm feeling mighty, mighty lank," said the sheriff. "Shooting at owlhoots always makes me hungry."

"You're just like me, Uncle Tom," she replied. "You can always find an excuse for eating. What it will end up doing to my figure!"

"I think it can stand quite a bit of 'doing' before you need start worrying," the sheriff said, with an appraising and approving glance. Dolores headed for the kitchen, making faces at him over her shoulder.

The result of her pilgrimage to the culinary domain was a repast to which all three did full justice regardless of the possibility of acquired poundage.

"And now," said Dolores, "I'm going to change and get ready to call it a night. The crowd is beginning to thin out. I wonder if we can have a peaceful day tomorrow, for a change."

"I hope so," Slade replied. "Day after tomorrow, General Manager Dunn will roll in, and I'd like to be in good shape for our conference."

"And I suppose some trouble will come

from that," Dolores sighed.

"I don't see any reason why there should," Slade differed.

"There will be if you run true to form," retorted the pessimist. "Let you out of my sight for a minute and you're into something." She flounced off to the dressing room, leaving Slade and the sheriff chuckling.

"Think Selby will slip back into town tonight?" the sheriff asked.

"Nothing to deter him if he wishes to," Slade answered. "Only he won't slip in, tonight or tomorrow. He'll ride in bold as brass, for his alibi is perfect." The sheriff said things under his mustache.

"Oh, he's a smart one," Slade said. "I doubt if we have ever gone up against a smarter. Well, we'll see."

"Here comes your gal," Calder remarked. "Guess we can call it a night."

13

Dolores got her wish, a quiet and peaceful day and night. And the following morning a long green-and-gold splendor with WI-NONA stenciled on the sides rolled into the railroad yards and ground to a stop on a spur track — General Manager Dunn's private car.

When Slade and the sheriff approached the private car, a couple of hours before noon, Sam, Dunn's combination porter, chef, and general factotum, who was standing on the rear platform, let out a joyous whoop.

"Here he is, boss!" he shouted. "Here's Mister Slade!"

"Bring him in!" boomed from the drawing room of the coach. "Break out a bottle, and fix a snack."

Slade and the old colored man, friends of long standing, shook hands and Sam led the way into the car where, behind his massive desk, was Jaggers Dunn, a massive man. He also had a warm greeting for *El Halcón,* and for the sheriff also, whom he knew well.

"Take a load off your feet," said Jaggers. "What's he been getting into since I saw him last, Calder?"

"Plenty," replied the sheriff. "Would take the rest of the morning to tell you about everything."

"We'll let it go, then," chuckled the magnate. "What *you* got to tell me, Walt?"

"Have something to show you that I think will interest you," Slade replied evasively, but with a smile. "Suppose you take a little ride with Tom and me."

"Okay," agreed the G.M. "After we finish our snack."

"Plenty of time," Slade assured him.

The snack proved very tasty and they lingered over it, with a snort for Calder and coffee for Slade, then repaired to Shadow's stable, where Agosta had a sturdy roan ready for Dunn, who swung himself into the saddle with a lightness and ease that many younger men might have envied. The thoughtful Agosta had also provided boots and spurs for his convenience. Leaving the stable, they rode to the river trail and turned west.

As a matter of habit, Slade was watchful and alert, although it was highly improbable anything would be tried against them in broad daylight. They passed the little towns, Santa Rita, La Paloma, Los Indios, Progresso, Santa Maria, and finally reached the Circle C holding where Slade led the way north.

"And here, sir, is the land you'll want for your assembly yards," he said, "and about thirty miles of your right-of-way, all at what you consider a fair price."

Dunn shook his head resignedly. "I don't know what I'd do without you," he sighed. "You can get more done in less time than anybody I know or ever heard of. This is perfect. I couldn't ask for better. And of course you have arranged things so that there'll be no difficulty swinging the deal with the owners of the property?"

"I venture to trust so," Slade replied.

"Then there's nothing to worry about where that angle is concerned," Dunn said.

"Like to keep on riding for a spell and look things over?" Slade asked. Dunn signified that he would.

So they rode on through the golden sunshine, and with every mile covered, Dunn grew more and more enthusiastic.

"Yes, this is plumb fine, better than anything I'd hoped for," he declared. "Usually the closer a line reaches the terminus, the greater the difficulties, but this is just the reverse. A minimum of grading, a minimum of curves, a minimum of ballast. We can erect a pumping station on the banks of that creek over there, which will cost less to build than it would to draw the water from the river, and will ensure a steady supply independent of the vagaries of the Rio Grande. With that blasted river, your intakes are liable to be left high and dry at any time. This is perfect."

Finally Slade glanced at the westering sun. "Guess we'd better be turning around and heading for home," he said. "As is, it will be past dark when we reach town, and I'd like for Boyer and Sefton to meet with Mr. Dunn and talk things over."

"A notion, all right," said Jaggers. "Let's go."

Now Slade was even more watchful, constantly scanning the terrain ahead, for he was experiencing an uneasy presentiment that trouble was brewing.

Because Dunn wished to check the course of the stream that flowed the heavy brush stands that flanked the west edge of the Circle C, and on that great bristle of chaparral Slade's attention was focused; it could afford concealment for all the outlaws in Texas.

The miles rolled by and now the sun was nearing the horizon and the east-west trail was no great distance ahead. Slade relaxed a little.

Then abruptly he tensed to hair-trigger alertness and slowed Shadow's pace slightly.

"Well," he remarked. "Looks like an attempt at a drygulching is in the works."

"What! What!" barked the sheriff.

"Look ahead about eight hundred yards," Slade said. "See the bird swooping and zooming over that particularly tall stand of brush, never settling?"

"I can see what looks like a speck of dust bouncing around in the air down there, but I wouldn't venture to say it's a bird," remarked Dunn, puckering his lids. "Those eyes of yours!"

"It's a bird, all right, a bluejay," Slade replied. "He's a cantankerous critter, but his kind has been a good friend to me more than once. He doesn't like anybody hanging around close under his nest or his perch, and tells the world so. A little closer and you can hear him screeching."

"Wouldn't be a wolf, or snake?"

Slade shook his head. "He'd pay a wolf no mind, and he'd peck the eyes out of a snake if it came too close, which it wouldn't. No, it is something he doesn't understand, and fears. In other words — man. Well, it must have been tedious waiting for us to ride back this way, so we'll endeavor to relieve the monotony for those gents with notions holed up in the brush."

He slid his heavy Winchester from the saddle boot as he spoke.

"Remember it, sir?" he said to Dunn. "The high-power, long-range special, point-blank to five hundred yards, that you had the gun people make to order for me. Keep on riding for a couple of hundred yards more or so." A few more minutes and he said,

"Now cut east right across the range; that should bring them into the open. What they don't know is that I have them decidedly out-ranged."

The horses' heads were turned due east, their pace quickened a little. Slade scanned the brush stand intently, and was not at all surprised when four horsemen bulged from the growth, spurring their mounts. Another moment and he clamped the Winchester butt to his shoulder.

The big rifle boomed. A hat went flying through the air.

"A little more wind than I thought," he

remarked, shifting the black muzzle a trifle.

Again the booming report, slamming its echo back from the brush. This time a man lurched in his saddle, slumped forward, clutching the saddle horn for support. Answering slugs whined past, none close, for the range was great for the average marksman.

A third bellow from the Winchester. An arm flew up wildly, dropped limp.

That was enough for the drygulchers. They whirled their horses and sped back the way they had come as a final bullet from the Winchester took its toll, through the top of a shoulder, Slade believed. Before he could fire again, all four, the wounded men managing to stay in their saddles, vanished into the chaparral.

"That should hold them, I'd say," Slade remarked cheerfully as he reloaded.

"If it doesn't, they're darn hard to satisfy," grunted Dunn. "Talk about shooting! Nigh seven hundred yards if an inch. Gentlemen, hush!" Slade laughed and turned Shadow's nose south.

With no further signs of the discomfited drygulchers, they reached the trail and headed for Brownsville. Slade was still watchful, but they reached town without misadventure. The horses were cared for.

Slade and the G.M. repaired to the private car, where Sam at once began preparing dinner. The sheriff hurried off to locate Boyer and Sefton.

"Have them give us an hour or so to eat, and hustle back yourself," Dunn directed.

Slade and the sheriff enjoyed a leisurely dinner with Dunn and were smoking and chatting when Boyer and Sefton arrived and were introduced. The General Manager proceeded to outline his proposition, much to their surprise.

"Never thought of such a thing, but it sure sounds all right to me," Boyer said when the magnate paused. "What do you say, Walt?"

"I believe you would do well to make the deal with Mr. Dunn," Slade replied.

"Then that settles it," said Boyer. Sefton voiced hearty accord. He looked a trifle dazed when Dunn named the amount he was ready to pay for the right-of-way and the land for the assembly yard. So did Boyer, for that matter.

"Why — why, Mr. Dunn, that is certainly generous of you," he said.

"Never mind that," Dunn replied brusquely. "I'm getting my money's worth."

"And we're getting a heck of a lot more than we ever expected to realize for the spread."

"And you'll still have enough land to take care of a sizeable herd of cows," Slade put in.

"Guess this is our lucky day, eh, Vibart?" Boyer declared.

"You're right," replied Sefton, adding, "and I know darn well who to thank for it," with a significant glance at *El Halcón*.

"Oh, he's always getting folks beholden to him," said Jaggers. "Just made that way, I guess." The sheriff nodded sober agreement.

"All right, now, to mention the matter to folks?" Boyer asked.

"Sure," answered the G.M. "No secret any longer."

"And it'll sure make folks sit up and notice," predicted Boyer. "The road coming through this way will mean a lot to Brownsville."

Dunn had come prepared to do business and the necessary papers were quickly drawn up; Sefton's being a lawyer expedited matters.

They talked for a while longer, then Dunn said:

"Well, gents, I guess we'll have to say so long for the present — *hasta luego,* as our Mexican brothers say. The night express is picking up my car in less than an hour. Got

167

to be in Chicago for a directors' meeting next week."

They shook hands all around, including Sam, the porter-chef, who was thanked for the prime surrounding he dished up. Slade and the others headed for the Blue Bell, where soon there was excitement aplenty as Boyer and Sefton spread the word of the coming of the railroad line from the north and the deal they'd made with Jaggers Dunn.

"And now I reckon we'd better amble across the bridge for a word with folks there," remarked Calder.

"A good notion," Slade agreed. "Estevan and his boys will have notified them that we are safe back in town, but they'll be anxious for details."

"Anyhow, you gave those hellions something to remember you by," Calder chuckled. "Three of 'em with punctured hides."

"Superficial wounds, I'd say," Slade replied. "And again I underestimated Selby's cunning. Somehow he figured where we were headed and laid his trap accordingly."

"Think he might somehow have known something of Mr. Dunn's plans and knew when he rode out with us it was to look over the Circle C holding?"

"I wouldn't put anything past him," answered Slade wearily. "He seems able to learn anything he desires to."

"And the devil is sure after you," growled Calder.

"But so far hasn't had any luck catching up," *El Halcón* rejoined. "And that's all that counts."

Matamoros was rather quiet, doubtless still trying to recover from the *fiesta* celebration, but when they reached La Luz, they found the cantina well crowded. Dolores, Estevan, and Amado at once joined them and were regaled with an account of the incidents of the day, Calder doing most of the talking.

Dolores shook her head at Slade. Estevan looked disgruntled at having missed the fun. Amado smiled broadly.

"Is for business most excellent," he said. "And I am glad for the *Señor* Sefton. He a good hombre is. With the golden wine we celebrate will." He beckoned a waiter, who hurried away, to reappear with bottles and crystal goblets he filled to the brim. Also a snort of redeye for the sheriff, and coffee for Slade.

"All the girls like Mr. Sefton," Dolores put in. "He's always courteous and considerate on the floor. Yes, we all think well of him."

"And that counts for plenty," said Slade. "Hard enough for a man to fool one woman, much less a dozen."

"The voice of experience speaks," said Dolores. She scampered off to the dance floor. The sheriff shook with laughter.

14

However, the sheriff didn't laugh long, for neither he nor Slade was in much of a mood for mirth. Hanging over was not only the threat of personal harm but the even more disturbing likelihood that some innocent person or persons would know death's sharpness. There was little doubt but that Mostyn Selby was in a killer mood and ready to vent his spleen on anyone who might cross his path. And what in blazes to do about it, neither had the slightest idea.

Estevan emptied his glass, bowed to Slade and strolled out. The sheriff's eyes followed him to the swinging doors.

"Maybe *he* will hit on something," he remarked hopefully.

Slade felt that the knife man might well do just that. Not much went on but that Estevan quickly knew it. And that Selby would be in action soon Slade was convinced. Well, at the moment all they could do was await developments and hope for the best. He shrugged his shoulders and ordered more coffee. Nothing gained by beating his brains out against imponderables. Things always had worked out and doubtless would again. When Dolores came over and wanted to dance, he welcomed the diversion.

They had several numbers together and when Slade returned to the sheriff, he was in a more complacent mood. An hour or so passed and Estevan returned, his eyes glowing with eagerness.

"Capitán," he said, "in his cantina the *ladrone* Selby is. With two of those five who rode with him west the other night. Standing nearby, pretending rather drunk to be, was an *amigo* of mine, not young, who looks older than he is, and also looks stupid, which he is not. Some of the talk he could hear and from it learned tomorrow the *ladrones* ride north."

"Did he learn to where they ride?" Slade asked quickly.

"The *ladrone* Selby said 'Far on the Alice road,' " Estevan replied.

"Far on the Alice Road!" repeated Calder. "I'll say they could ride far on the Alice Road, as some folks call that trail. It starts here on Jackson Street and turns due north

172

for about a hundred and seventy miles to Alice. You sure that was what was said, Estevan?"

"My *amigo* makes not the mistake," Estevan answered. "Far on the Alice Road is what the *ladrone* said." The sheriff started another protest, but Slade interrupted.

"Tom," he said, "I think the old *amigo* heard right and repeated right, but did not interpret right, no reason why he should. What Selby said was not 'far' — f-a-r — on the Alice road, but Pharr — P-h-a-r-r, the town of Pharr, which is on the road to Alice, around fifty miles north of here, perhaps a trifle more."

"By gosh, you've hit it!" the sheriff exclaimed excitedly. "The town of Pharr. Incidentally, a stage still runs from Alice to Brownsville."

"And lays over for the night at Pharr," Slade said.

"And that's right, too," Calder agreed. "Say! Things are beginning to tie up."

"Begins to look a little that way," Slade conceded.

"And you figure the devils might make a try for that stage, which does pack considerable *dinero* at times?"

"I can't see, at least at the moment, what other reason they'd have for taking a fifty-

173

mile ride," Slade replied.

"And I guess we'll be taking a fifty-mile ride, too," Calder said cheerfully.

"About the size of it, I reckon," Slade smiled. Estevan also smiled, and fondled the haft of his throwing blade.

"So, have your boys keep close watch on the devils, Estevan," Slade said, "and when they ride out of town tomorrow, let us know at once."

"*Capitán,* it will be done," Estevan promised. He drained his glass and drifted out. The sheriff contemplated Slade.

"Looks sorta good, wouldn't you say?" he remarked.

"Yes, it does, on the surface at least," *El Halcón* replied. "To all appearances the outfit is going to make a play for something at or near Pharr, and of course the stage from Alice is the logical objective. But that smart devil has pulled so many unexpected rabbits from the hat that I'm leery of everything he has a hand in."

"Now don't you go getting pessimistic," chuckled Calder.

"I'm not," Slade said smilingly. "I'm confident we'll make out. But I do wish Estevan's old friend had overheard a bit more of the conversation. Undoubtedly, Selby was giving his hellions instructions. If we knew what they were, we'd really know how to drop a loop on the bunch. Well, we'll see."

"Here comes your gal, and she looks suspicious," the sheriff said.

"So, still here," Dolores voiced the obvious as she plumped into a chair beside Slade. "When Estevan hurried in, I felt sure you were off on another gallivanting."

"Not tonight, unless something very unexpected happens," he reassured her. "It's getting late," he added, with a glance at the clock.

"And I'm going to change," she said. "We'll try and get out of here before something does happen." She trotted to the dressing room.

"Wonder what time those devils will leave town tomorrow," the sheriff remarked.

"Fairly early, I hope, and I think they will. They'll have a long ride ahead of them, and it is logical to believe they won't push their horses too much, wishing to keep them fairly fresh in case of need. Yes, I hope they leave before noon, or very shortly after. I plan to let them get several hours start on us. If we ride out right after they do, it will notify anybody keeping tabs on us that we're following their trail, and Selby may have made provisions against that."

"Guess that's right," Calder agreed.

"Would be just like the horned toad. Well, here comes your gal, all dressed up for the street. And here comes Estevan."

Dolores paused to speak with Amado. Estevan approached the table.

"The other three of the five who rode west that night joined the two in the *ladrone's,*" he said. "They talked. What they said was not heard. Then the five to that small hotel on Elizabeth Street went. The *ladrone* Selby in the cantina remained."

Slade digested this bit of information for a few minutes, then said:

"Okay, call your boys off; the devils are bedded down for the night. But have the *amigos* back on the job a few hours after daybreak, ready to report on the movements of the five. Okay?"

"*Capitán,* as you say it shall be done," replied Estevan. He sauntered out. Dolores said goodnight to Amado and joined Slade.

An hour before noon, Slade, Calder, and the deputies, Gus and Webley, were sitting in the office when Estevan appeared. He wasted no words.

"The five rode north and east by way of Jackson Street," he said. "The *cabron* Selby was with them not."

"Didn't expect him to ride out with

them," Slade replied. "He will join them somewhere along the way. Webley, you and Gus go circulate around where everybody can see you. Keep away from them, Estevan, but wander about in plain sight. We meet at Agosto's stable at two o'clock. Everything understood?"

The others nodded, and one by one they drifted out.

"Looks like everything is going smoothly so far," observed Calder.

"Yes, looks that way," Slade conceded. "I wish I knew for sure Selby's whereabouts, but I believe I'm right in my opinion that he will join the others some miles north of here. Hope I *am* right, and that he hasn't guessed our little plan. In which case we might run into a disagreeable surprise somewhere."

"I don't see you ambling into any trap no matter how smooth it's set," said the sheriff. "But suppose we do amble over to the Blue Bell and tie onto a surrounding. No telling when we'll get another chance to eat."

"Guess I can put away a sandwich and a cup of coffee," Slade agreed. The sheriff smirked.

They took their time eating, chatted with Boyer for a while, went out and wandered about the streets, then repaired to Agosto's stable, where Estevan and the deputies awaited them, the horses saddled and bridled.

Twenty minutes later they were riding north in perfect Texas weather. The trees flaunted their sheen of green and gold against the deep blue of the sky. The grasses were ocean-ripples in the wind, great shadows rushing toward the horsemen, to vanish as by a magic touch.

Here there was little need of caution, for on the open prairie visibility stretched for miles. Later it would be different, through the brush country to the north where the outlaws rode.

A country well worth fighting for, to keep it clean and wholesome for honest men and women, free from the taint of greed and wanton cruelty personified by men like Mostyn Selby and his ruthless followers, Slade thought as he gazed upon the feast of beauty spread before his eyes. Texas! America!

The sun drifted down the long slant of the western sky. Vivid hues stained the flecks of cloud. The miles churned back under the horses' speeding irons. Ahead the stands of tall and thick chaparral loomed dark and ominous.

Slade grew more watchful. For several

miles, through the brush country, spots ideal for a drygulching were numerous. He did not think there was much danger of such a happening. Mostyn Selby, shrewd as he was, could hardly be omniscient, and he would have had to be, or very near it, to anticipate the posse's move.

He proved right so far as the brush belt was concerned. They passed through it without incident, with full darkness now close, and entered the region of cultivation. Citrus groves lined the trail in places, and fields of cotton and vegetables. There were also date and fan palms, and semi-tropical flowers, with here and there the gleam of water that marked a freshly irrigated tract.

"This is going to be quite a section before they get through with it," the sheriff remarked.

"Yes," Slade replied, "one of the richest. And already it is feeling the touch of modern progress. Not very far north of Pharr, toward Edinburg, is what will soon be one of the largest car-icing plants in the Southwest, for the handling of perishable fruits and vegetables on long hauls to distant markets. The coming of the railroad made that possible, of course, as Mr. Dunn's line to the south over the Circle C will make one possible down there. The wheels of progress keep turning, despite the efforts of such critters as Selby to slow them down and bring back what they term the good old days when the outlaw was supreme, or close to it."

They continued to ride under the glittering stars. Some miles farther on and they reached a stretch of uncultivated prairie.

"Here we turn east for a couple of miles, then north again; I wish to approach Pharr from the north, where there is plenty of cover, while there is none to the south of the town," Slade said.

"That makes sense," agreed Calder.

Now Slade was more than usually alert, for there was a chance the outlaws might have had a similar notion and had also ridden east to approach Pharr and the stage station from the chaparral-grown north.

As he rode, from a cunningly hidden pocket in his broad leather belt he slipped a gleaming silver star set on a silver circle — the feared and honored badge of the Texas Ranger, gazed at it a moment, then replaced it in the pocket.

"I believe I may still be able to get by on my deputy sheriff's badge without revealing my Ranger connections," he said. "I'd like to stay undercover in the section for a while longer, if possible. Anyhow, I have you all deputized and if questions happen to be asked, you are in the clear — you are peace officers in any part of Texas."

"You'll get by, all right," Calder predicted cheerfully. "I happen to know the sheriff of Hidalgo County, a right old jigger. He'll string along with us if necessary and say that even though we are from Cameron County, he's got us deputized."

"That helps," Slade said.

They rode on, and again Walt Slade thrilled to the vast panorama of beauty surrounding him. Under its calm majesty, his spirit sank to nothingness, but nevertheless was uplifted. For he was part, a tiny part, indeed, but still a part of the mighty whole.

Still, it behooved him to be humble. "Crass human!" murmured the little stream through which the horses splashed. "Crass human, you set yourself above me, who am but a runlet of water, but ages hence, when you are but a handful of gray dust, I will still be here, singing to the stars, smiling and jumping to the sun. Go to, with your vaunted dominion over all created things. Nay, man was made for the world, *not* the world for man!"

15

Another mile of fairly fast riding and Slade changed the course to north by slightly west, which would continue until they were past Pharr. Then a little more west, then due south through the chaparral to the stage station.

"Getting sorta late," the sheriff remarked. "I've a notion we'll have some action before long now."

"We should," Slade answered, "that is, if there is going to be any. A little more to the west; another ten minutes and we'll be passing Pharr."

His directions were followed and shortly his keen eyes made out the sprawling buildings of the car-icing plant beside the east-west railroad line. On a siding stood a long string of cars set for the icing.

The buildings were dark, save one, in which glowed a single light.

The posse rode on, slowing the pace. Soon

the car-icing plant fell behind as they neared Pharr.

"Right ahead," Slade said, "is a rise that is made to order for us. From its crest we can see for quite a distance in every direction. That's where we'll hole up till the devils show and are in the station."

"Hope the devils ain't on the rise ahead of us," muttered the sheriff.

"I'm sure they won't approach until the station is shut up and dark," Slade replied. "Isn't logical for them to do otherwise, taking the needless chance of being spotted. Let's go!"

The rise loomed before them. Without mishap they climbed the brushy slope to the crest. Slade uttered an exclamation of satisfaction.

"Stage is already in," he said. "Building all lit up. Soon the lights will be put out. If the stage is packing money, it will be placed in the station safe for the night. Now all we can do is take it easy and wait. I feel pretty sure the devils will approach from the west, and I'll see them quite a spell before they get here."

The wait was tedious, but finally things quieted down around the station, the lights winked out. Voices were heard calling good-nights. Slade concentrated on the west.

Another tedious wait, this one a bit hard on the nerves, being based on expectation. To the posse members it seemed quite a while before Slade said:

"Here they come, out of the west, and quite a little to the north. They'll turn south on the Alice trail. Get set!"

A few minutes more, and the sheriff said, "I can see 'em, too, six of the devils." Still a few more minutes, and he exclaimed,

"What the blazes! They've crossed the Alice trail and are riding straight east. Now what in heck does that mean?"

"It means we've been outsmarted," Slade replied bitterly. "It isn't the stage or the station they have in mind, but the car-icing plant. Must be money stashed there. Very likely in the room, no doubt the office, where the light is burning. All right, down off here and east for two or three hundred yards, and hope we're not spotted, then turn north and get as near that blasted plant as we can risk the horses. The rest of the way on foot, through the brush. With luck we should make it. But we're mighty sure to end up with a ripsnorting gunfight. No chance for poling a nice surprise as we would have if we had holed up inside the station like I planned."

"Fine!" said Calder. "I'm itchin' to line

sights with the blankety-blanks."

"Ha, the fun!" chorted Estevan, fingering his blade. The deputies also made blithe remarks suitable to the occasion. "Let's go!" Slade chuckled. They sped down the slope, reached the foot of it and raced east.

It was a nerve-wracking business, riding across the open prairie with the starlight bright enough to reveal large objects to hostile watching eyes. Even *El Halcón* breathed relief when, after whipping north, they reached the comparative shelter of the clumps of chaparral. He slowed the pace, veered west. He could catch glimpses of the car-icing plant, which was drawing steadily nearer. The buildings were still dark, save for that one subdued glow as of a turned-down lamp behind a window.

Another fifty yards or so and Slade called a halt. "This is as far as we can risk the horses," he said, keeping his voice very low. "Now it's on foot. Keep yours eyes and ears open. One little slip would very likely be our last. So don't make one."

They tethered the cayuses, hoping they would keep quiet, and stole slowly forward toward that glowing window, guns ready for instant action, Slade slightly to the front.

Abruptly he halted, with a whispered warning to the others. His unusual hearing had caught a sound, a faint, musical sound, the tinkle of bridle irons as a horse petulantly tossed its head. "They're here," he breathed to his companions. "Horses are in that thicket to the left. Hold it for a minute."

Scarcely daring to draw breath, conscious of the pounding of their own hearts, the posse stood motionless, peering and listening. Had the outlaws detected their stealthy approach and were they just waiting until they reached the point where an unexpected blast of gunfire would be most effective? That was the life or death question that confronted them.

But there was no further sound that even the ears of *El Halcón* could register. Taking a chance, he continued the slow advance. Now the lighted window was less than thirty yards distant.

Then abruptly there was another sound, a gasping cry that came from the direction of the building. A cry, then a mumble of voices.

Flinging caution to the winds, Slade raced forward, the others crowding after him, and reached a place where he could peer through the lighted window.

In the room, which was evidently an office, were seven men. One was tall, bearded. Five others had hatbrims pulled low, neckerchiefs drawn high.

The seventh man was an elderly individual with blood streaming down his face from a gashed scalp.

The bearded man gestured toward a big steel safe that stood against one wall. The old fellow, his eyes terrified, his face contorted with pain, lurched and shambled across the room, bent over the safe, clutching it for support, and with fumbling fingers began twirling the combination knob.

Slade took in the situation at a glance. Close to the window was a door that stood ajar. "Keep down!" he snapped to his companions. He bounded forward, hit the door with his shoulder and slammed it open. His great voice rolled in thunder through the room,

"Up! You are under arrest! In the name of the State of Texas!"

The room fairly exploded into hectic activity. Slade lined sights with the tall, bearded man, who already had his gun out. But before *El Halcón* could squeeze his trigger, the devil went sideways behind one of his companions, who took the slug intended for him. A bullet smashed the single bracket lamp and the room was plunged in darkness through which the orange flashes of the guns blazed.

There was the thud of a falling body,

another, and still another as Estevan's knife hissed through the smoke fog. There was a curse behind Slade, a gasp of pain; the outlaws were also taking their toll.

Feet beat the floor boards. Slade fired at the sound. His companions' guns bellowed. *El Halcón* surged forward, tripped over something and for a moment reeled off balance. He recovered but heard a door bang open as he leaped over what had tripped him. But by the time he reached the back door of the office, there was no one in sight. Thumbs hooked over the hammers of his Colts, he paused, listening intently.

From no great distance away came the muffled thud of horses' irons on the thick turf. Slade shot at the sound until the hammers of his guns clicked on empty shells. But the uproar of the posse's firing filtered the distancing beat of hoofs.

"Hold it!" Slade shouted. "Somebody get a light going, and shoot at anything that moves!"

A match flared, showing five motionless forms sprawled on the office floor. The match went out, but another flickered, then the soft glow of a bracket lamp, to the wick of which Calder had touched the match flame.

"Safe for me to move now?" a voice asked

from the floor.

"Guess so," Slade chuckled in reply to the old night watchman with the gashed scalp. "Looks like the lead has stopped flying, for the moment, at least."

The sheriff chortled his pleasure. "Collected us another bag of carcasses," he said.

"But again Selby got in the clear," Slade replied disgustedly. "I was sure I had him, but he moved like a flash of lightning, had another devil in front of him before I could shift my muzzle. And I'm ready to wager he shot out the light. Oh, well, maybe next time.

"Anybody badly hurt?" he asked anxiously.

"Oh, Webley got his arm nicked, nothing serious," Calder answered. "Gus got a sliver of meat knocked on his face, which will just make him even purtier than he already ain't."

Deciding the wounds were trifling, Slade said, "I'll take care of them shortly. Let's have a look at what we knocked off."

Said Estevan, wiping his blade on a dead outlaw's hair, "Four of the five who with the *ladrone* Selby rode. They ride no more."

Slade turned to the watchman. "And now perhaps you can line us up on just what was going on here," he suggested.

"The scuts were after the money in the safe, that's what," the watchman replied. "There's plenty in that box, to meet the payroll tomorrow — we got a large force of workers — and running expenses for the month. We've never had any trouble like this before. I'm on the job especially to keep an eye out for fire — we've had a couple in the past few years. That's how I happen to know the combination of the safe, so I can get the money out in case of fire. How *they* knew that, I don't know, but evidently they did. I was just getting ready to have my lunch when I heard the back door open — it was supposed to be locked. The devils rushed in. The big one with the whiskers batted me with the barrel of his sixshooter, not too hard, but hard enough to show me they meant business. Told me to open the safe. I didn't figure to arg'fy with the hellions.

"And," he added slowly, "I've a prime notion you fellers saved me from getting a punctured hide. Got a feeling they're the sort that don't leave witnesses."

"You're right," Slade said grimly. "And as for knowing you know the combination to the safe, they seem able to learn anything they wish to, like opening the supposed-to-be locked back door. Well, I hear folks whooping in Pharr, and headed this way.

190

They'll want to hear about what went on."

"And I want somebody to try and locate old Branch Tuttle, the sheriff of Hidalgo County," said Calder.

"Chances are he'll be the first to show up," said the watchman. "He was at a bar on Main Steet a little while ago."

As the shouts drew nearer, Slade went out and whistled for Shadow, who came in answer to his call, snorting inquiringly. Securing his medicants from the saddle bags, Slade treated the deputies' superficial wounds.

"That should hold you," he told Gus, giving a final pat to a pad he taped in place, Webley having already been cared for.

The watchman wasn't far wrong. Among the first to arrive from town was bulky, keen-eyed old Sheriff Branch Tuttle, who did not appear particularly surprised by what had happened. In fact, Slade thought, he was about as difficult to surprise as Estevan.

"Always figured something like this would happen to these out-of-the-way shacks," he observed. "Understand that after a bit they plan to move 'em farther north, into Edinburg, where there'll be folks around all the time."

"We sorta horned in on your preserves,

Branch," said Calder. "Well, there's some carcasses for you to play with."

"Take 'em to Brownsville and put 'em on display," replied Tuttle. He lowered a lid at *El Halcón,* who smiled his understanding.

"Reckon Deputy Slade packs enough authority to handle things," he added. "And now you fellers better come along with me for a surrounding and a whack of ear pounding. We'll take care of the cayuses, too."

"Found the ones those devils rode tied in the brush," put in Webley.

"They can pack the carcasses to Brownsville," said Tuttle. "Reckon the car-icing people will have something nice to say to you fellers."

"Slade gets most of the credit," replied Calder. "It was him figured things out."

"Per usual," said Tuttle. "Let's go."

After a hearty meal and a refreshing sleep, the posse set out for town through the golden glow of mid-morning. Progress, with the awkwardly burdened outlaw horses, was slow and the west was aflame with sunset when they reached Brownsville, to the accompaniment of more than a little excitement as they jogged down Jackson Street and to the sheriff's office. Calder complacently surveyed the bodies laid out on the floor.

"I sorta cater to those decorations," he said. "Look real pretty there. Okay, Gus, let folks in to look 'em over."

The dead outlaws were examined with much the usual results. Several citizens were sure they'd seen one or more of the bunch in various parts of town but didn't remember anything outstanding about them. Which did not surprise Slade, and he was but mildly interested, anyhow. They had been just hired hands. Mostyn Selby was his objective and all else mattered little.

"Wouldn't you figure we've just about cleaned up the devil's outfit?" Calder remarked after he shooed out the loiterers and locked the door.

"One would think so," Slade replied. "But undoubtedly it was a big outfit to start with, and if he feels the need of them, he can always get more. That is, if he's able to make successful raids, as it appeared he was doing until recently. Owlhoots flock to a leader who can produce results."

"You're right," growled the sheriff, "and there are plenty here abouts to do the flocking. To heck with 'em right now! I'm hungry; let's go eat. The Blue Bell, or across the river to Amado's cantina?"

"I think we'll stand a better chance of not being pestered across the river," Slade decided.

"Guess that's so," Calder agreed. " 'Spect the little gal will want to have dinner with us; reckon she had to eat her breakfast alone."

"Logical to assume so, seeing as she lives alone," Slade replied smilingly. The sheriff snickered under his mustache.

Without misadventure, they crossed the bridge and reached the cantina. Dolores was the first to greet them, with Amado close behind.

"Seems as goes the saying, *Capitán,* you the hell raised up and under the corner shoved the chunk," he said.

"I had help," Slade answered. "It was a rather lively go while it lasted."

"So said Estevan," Amado chuckled. "He the kitchen in is, telling the help all, and how his blade drank deep."

"It did that, all right," Slade conceded. "He appears to handle it as well in the dark as in the light."

"The eye of the Yaqui, even as *Capitán's,* in the dark sees," said Amado.

"Won't you two please switch to something pleasant," Dolores chided. "I'm hungry."

"Ha!" said Amado, and hurried to the kitchen.

It took the cook quite a while to prepare their dinner, but when it arrived, all agreed that it was worth waiting for. After dinner Dolores retired to the back room and some paper work, Amado to his post at the far end of the bar. Slade and the sheriff were left to discuss matters.

"Yes, there's no doubt but that Selby will be on the move soon," the Ranger said. "He's had too many setbacks of late to make it feasible for him to be idle long. His followers, what's left of them, must be getting quite short of spending money, something no owlhoot bunch will tolerate for any length of time. They'll begin branching out on their own and, lacking his brains, bring the roof falling in on them in a hurry."

"His brains ain't been doing him over much good of late," Calder commented. "Of course, though, there are brains *and* brains, as I've a notion he's realizing about now."

"Thank you," Slade smiled, "but I'm not particularly proud of the way they've been functioning at times of late. It seems to me he has steadily been a jump ahead of me. Like the car-icing chore last night. He did the last thing I'd have figured on him doing."

"You came out on top, and that's all that really counts," the sheriff said cheerfully.

"I figure I got the breaks," Slade replied.

"Uh-huh, like figuring in a split second the right thing to do and how to do it."

"Not too bad, I guess, for past performance," Slade conceded. "But now we have to deal with the present and the future, and I've not the slightest idea, at present, how the cards are going to fall."

The sheriff was optimistic. "I got a strong feeling," he said, "that the game is darn near over. Mighty soon, I figure, we'll be leveling off the chips, dropping the decks in the drawer, and looking forward to another and different session."

Slade laughed at the rather far-fetched conceit of likening his conflict with the outlaws to a card game, but hoped the sheriff was right in his conclusions, and that he, Slade, would deal the last hand.

Dolores joined them and asked for a glass of wine, which she sipped daintily.

"Think you'll be able to stay put and keep out of trouble for tonight?" she asked.

"After what happened last night, I'd say there's a good chance of it," Slade replied.

"Yep, got a notion the hellions will still be lickin' their wounds," the sheriff put in. "Reckon they're still trying to figure what

196

hit 'em. They sure were taken by surprise."

"So were we, but not so seriously," Slade said. "We were able to counter with the old saying that the best defense is a good offense. At least it worked out that way."

16

Dolores got her wish. The night passed uneventfully with business in the cantina good but not outstanding.

"And there shouldn't be much going on tomorrow night," she remarked when she returned from changing. "Tonight, rather, for it's nearly daylight. For tomorrow, or the next day, whichever you wish to call it, is payday for the railroads and the docks, and most of the ranches, too."

"By gosh, that's right," said the sheriff. "What with one thing and another, I plumb forgot about it. Yep, we can use a day of quiet today, for it sure won't be quiet tomorrow. Most anything liable to happen."

When Amado was sounding his last call, Estevan appeared and accepted a last drink, and said, laconically as usual, of Selby:

"In his cantina he was. To the hotel where he sleeps went he. Did not reappear. I told my *amigos* to a night call it."

"Right," Slade replied. "He's gone to bed and we'd better emulate his example. As Dolores says, build up our strength against payday. Chances are we'll need it."

Payday dawn gave promise of fine weather for the coming celebration. A celebration it would be, the payday bust in a border town. A brief surcease from toil and problems, a wholehearted fling of hectic enjoyment.

The railroad paycar rolled in on time, the barred window was flung up and the paymaster began handing out the filled envelopes to the long file of railroaders (the various roads used the same car in the interest of economy and safety).

The dock workers and others were being paid, and cowhands from the nearer spreads were already riding in, hitching their horses to the racks and diving into the nearest saloon. Over the swinging doors came laughter and talk, snatches of song, or what was apparently intended for it, and occasional whoops, which would become more frequent as the redeye began getting in its licks.

The weather was warm and pleasant, with just enough breeze to temper the heat and fling up spurtles of dust under the beat of the horses' irons.

Payday! The big day of the month, with everybody, including the town folks, combining to make it a success.

"Liable to be too darn much of a success before all is said and done," thought Sheriff Tom Calder as he swore in several special deputies to help keep something like order.

"Yep, she's going to be a wild one," he said.

"I fear you're right," Slade conceded as he gazed out the window at the crowded street. "The boys are beginning to whoop it up quite early."

"Think our *amigo* Selby may try to make something of it?" Calder asked.

"Not beyond the realm of the possible," *El Halcón* replied. "There is going to be a lot of loose money floating around tonight, and a lot concentrated in certain spots. He may well believe that opportunity is in the making for him. And it may well be. Up to us to try and do a little anticipating."

"If the paycar was being held over here tonight, I'd say the devil might make a try for that," observed the sheriff. "Be plenty of money in that car, to pay off at Laredo, Sanderson, El Paso. But they're going to hook her onto the afternoon westbound express."

"Yes, that's out," Slade agreed. "Well, I

think I'll go stroll around for a while. Things are lively and interesting."

"Okay," replied Calder, "but watch your step and keep your eyes skun. Don't look like the hellion would try something against you in broad daylight on crowded streets, but blast him! He is uncanny. Reckon your old Scottish great-grandmother would hold he's got the second sight."

"That I rather doubt," Slade said laughingly, "but I agree with you that he'll sure bear watching. Be seeing you."

Slade did find the streets interesting and plenty lively. He sauntered about, visited various places, replied to greetings, studied faces and listened to conversations, and saw or heard nothing he considered of importance.

The hours jogged along to the unbelievable beauty of the sunset, and now Brownsville was really beginning to howl. As the lovely blue dusk sifted down from the star-flecked sky, he crossed the bridge and made his way to La Luz.

The cantina was jam-packed for fair. Dolores joined him, bright-eyed and vivacious.

"Yes, it's a wild one," she said, "but I'm enjoying every minute of it. And I'll keep on enjoying it if you will stick around and refrain from getting into trouble."

"Nothing in the offing so far," he reassured her. "Looks like folks are all having too good a time to go in for really serious hell-raising."

"I sure hope so," she replied. "We've had a few scuffles, but that's all. The boys took care of them pronto. Well, back to the floor for a while." She trotted off, casting him a smile over her shoulder, the spangles on her short skirt catching the light, the sway of her hips catching appreciative glances.

Estevan strolled in and accepted a chair and a glass of wine.

"He in his cantina is," he remarked, referring to Mostyn Selby. "When my wine I finish, and a bite in the kitchen, back to watch I go. For any move he makes I prepare and will *Capitán* tell at once."

But even Estevan slightly underestimated Mostyn Selby's cunning.

Dolores skipped back from the floor for a moment. "I've ordered dinner for both of us," she said. "Hope you're hungry."

"Well, has been quite a while since breakfast, has it not?" he countered.

"I suppose so," she replied demurely and flounced off.

The cook took his time preparing a dinner he considered fitting to the occasion, and when it finally did arrive, breakfast or no breakfast, both did it full justice.

Meanwhile, in the dark mouth of a narrow alley, little more than a crack between two buildings, diagonally across from Mostyn Selby's Albemarle saloon, Estevan lounged comfortably. He could catch glimpses of Selby moving about, chatting with customers, directing the activities of waiters and floor men. Looked like he would be occupied for the night, for business in the Albemarle was booming.

However, Estevan waas taking no chances with him, and kept an unceasing watch. He shifted to a still more comfortable position — and then whirled, his long blade flickering out, as he heard a slight sound behind him and saw the downward-slashing knife meant for his back. There was a clash of steel on steel, and instantly Estevan knew he was up against an experienced and skillful knife fighter.

It was cut and parry, slash and riposte, the shimmering blades catching the light. The grim opponents fighting in silence save for the gasping pant of their breathing. A single false move meant death, and both knew it.

The end came quickly. Estevan flung up his left arm, took the other's blade in it. His own steel drove forward.

Blood gushed over his hand. There was a choking, gurgling cry and his adversary reeled back and fell.

Estevan leaped over the still-twitching body and sped up the alley, tightening his neckerchief over his own profusely bleeding arm. He had the bleeding pretty well under control by the time he reached the lighted streets and attracted no attention. He quickly crossed the bridge and approached La Luz by way of the alley that paralleled the cantina. The cook opened the back door in answer to his tapped signal.

"What happen — yourself cut?" he asked, gazing at the bloody neckerchief.

Estevan told him briefly. "Fetch *Capitán*," he concluded, then said a few words in Spanish to one of the helpers, who at once slid out the back door.

The cook opened the door into the bar room a crack, nodded to Slade, who nodded back and strolled to the kitchen. He inspected the knife wound.

"Get medicants from the back room," he ordered.

"It is the scratch only," Estevan deprecated the wound.

"*Si,* a scratch that needs to be taken care of," Slade said and went to work on the

204

injury, smearing it with antiseptic salve, padding and bandaging it.

"Now tell me how you got it," he said. Estevan did so.

"So the cunning devil caught on you were keeping tabs on him from the alley mouth and set his own nice little trap to eliminate you," *El Halcón* remarked. "Oh, he's a shrewd one, all right, as I believe I mentioned before."

"I sent word to *amigos* two," Estevan said. "They will over the chore take."

"And you try and take it easy, and give that arm a chance," Slade ordered. "Nothing to it if it's cared for, just a slice through the flesh, but could give you trouble if neglected.

"Well, guess the sheriff will be dropping in shortly. The body will have been discovered and reported to him. He'll know very well whose handiwork was involved and will wish to hear just what did happen. We'll let other folks do some guessing. Now you go in and keep Dolores company. Sure you can have some wine. Will be good for you, having lost some blood."

Confident the rugged half-Yaqui would suffer no ill from the injury, he chatted with the cook and his helpers for a while and then repaired to the table to await the sheriff's arrival.

Calder dropped in shortly and glanced inquiringly at Estevan. The knife man repeated his laconic explanation. The sheriff chuckled.

"Wouldn't be surprised if the hellion is wondering how it happened to his knife-in-the-back devil. He must have been picked special for the chore. Wonder where he got him?"

"Knife fighters are not particularly uncommon," Slade said. "It's a hobby with certain individuals, in the nature of a game. Of course now and then there is a killer among them, especially the more skillful. They seem to develop an urge to use their skill in a lethal manner. That one showed bad judgment in picking his target."

"Darn bad," grunted the sheriff, sampling his snort. "He'll know better next time."

"But not in this world," Slade smiled. "Estevan plays for keeps."

"Think Selby may make a try at something tonight?" the sheriff asked.

"Things being as they are, one would be inclined to say no," Slade replied. "But he is utterly unpredictable and may have something in mind. But what? — that's your question. You find the answer for us."

"You're supposed to be the brains of this

outfit," Calder pointed out. "I just go along for the ride."

"And what bothers me is the chance I may be taken for a ride, speaking in the idiom," Slade answered.

"Whatever that last means," grunted the sheriff. "But if there's any 'riding' to be done, you'll be in the saddle, no doubt in my mind as to that."

"Here's hoping," Slade said, and ordered more coffee, and the sheriff a snort with which to keep him company.

Now the payday bust was really getting under way. Outside, on the street, was a continual chatter of voices, interspersed with whoops and snatches of song. The high-pitched laughter of women sounded above the gruffer tones of men, for dance floor girls had slipped out of the various cantinas with their escorts, presumably for a breath of fresh air.

"And this ain't nothing to what it must be north of the river," remarked Calder. "Don't you figure we'd better mosey across after a bit, to see how the deputies are making out?"

"Yes," Slade replied. "We will shortly. Estevan, the cook's motioning to you."

Estevan glided to the kitchen; he was back very quickly.

"While I away from the alley was, the *ladrone* out slipped," he reported the word from one of his *amigos*. "In his cantina he is not."

The sheriff swore explosively. Slade looked grave.

"Yes, we'd better cross the river," he said. "Looks like the devil is up to some hellishness. Perhaps we can learn something in Brownsville. You stay here, Estevan, and take care of that arm. And don't go blaming yourself for his escape. There was nothing you could have done about it. You did exactly the right thing. Otherwise you might have lost more blood than would have been good for you. Be seeing you soon. Tell Dolores we're just taking a walk across the bridge."

After a good deal of good-natured shoving and jostling, they reached the bridge and crossed it warily, for there was no telling what Selby might be up to, and Slade was taking no chances with the cunning devil.

However, they reached the north shore without misadventure, threaded their way through the crowded streets and ultimately reached the sheriff's office, where Deputy Webley was contemplating with satisfaction the body laid out on the floor.

"Ornery-looking specimen, wouldn't you

say?" the sheriff remarked to Slade.

"Oh, about the same as we've been collecting," *El Halcón* replied. "Stringy, well muscled, doubtless was quick as a cat on his feet; would very likely have done for anybody other than Estevan, who has no peer when it comes to knife work."

"Didn't have much money on him," Calder observed. "Yep, got a notion our *amigo* Selby is just about scraping the bottom of his *dinero* barrel. And I guess that means he'll be getting busy mighty soon."

"Definitely," Slade replied, his face grim. "Well, suppose we take a look at the Blue Bell; Boyer might have something to tell us."

"Okay," agreed the sheriff. "Web, you stick around the office till Gus or one of the specials relieves you. Anything much happened so far?"

"Not so far," replied the deputy. "A few friendly ruckuses that never really got going. But by the way the hellions are putting away the redeye, anything's liable to happen."

It took a good deal of pushing and jostling to reach the Blue Bell, but they finally made it. They found the big room hazy with smoke, the roof beams quivering with the noise, for the uproar was something to write home about, as the sheriff put it. Boyer greeted them warmly.

"Darn nigh had to fight to hold your table open," he said. "Blazes, what a night! I never saw its equal. Seems everybody all the way from Port Isabel to Laredo and points east and west is in town."

"And do you hate it!" snorted Calder sarcastically. "Listen to that till bell! And every time it rings you smirk. Oh, to be a rumhole owner and get rich!"

Boyer chuckled, and didn't argue the point. The sheriff accepted a snort on the house. Slade settled for coffee.

Slade gazed around the roaring room and shook his head. The scene was unreal, livid, medieval. It made him think of a dance of Apaches after a victory of massacre and lust. Or a dance of primitives, stark elementals who romped with ghouls and goblins damned under an orbed moon.

However, he knew it was but a passing phase. Come tomorrow and these revelers and their incredible hilarity would again be staid and sober workers and shopkeepers, expertly handling their various chores. But tonight! Payday in a border town!

"Well, if Selby don't make something of this, he's lost his magic touch," declared the sheriff. "Money everywhere, rumholes burstin' with it."

"But they've all hired extra guards to keep an eye on it," Slade said. "You can rely on it, that if he does make a try for something, it will be original, unique. That's just what I'm afraid of, and don't know what to do about it."

"Just take it easy and don't worry," advised Calder. "Right along you've been doing as much as anybody could expect of you, and doing all right, too. Things will work out, they always do. Waiter!"

Slade conceded it was sound advice and proceeded to adopt it. And he knew that, even if he did voice disapproval of the antics taking place, that he was enjoying the wild hullabaloo. And for that matter, so was the rugged old sheriff, despite his grunts and snorts. The gleam in his frosty eyes was not reflected from the lamps. Tom Calder thrived on excitement.

But Slade was not wrong when he maintained that if Mostyn Selby pulled a chore it would be unique, out of the ordinary and most unexpected. Selby did just that.

17

Old Owen Barnes was a cattle buyer, and a big one. Some folks insisted he was eccentric, but in reality, his eccentricities, so-called, were based on sound common sense and an exhaustive knowledge of the weaknesses of men.

It was said of Shanghai Pierce, also a buyer, among many other things, that when his wagon rolled the musical clinking of the silver quarters and half-dollars with which it was loaded could be heard when a mile away. And it was true.

No silvery clinking resounded from Owen Barnes' buckboard. For Barnes dealt only in "folding" money, of which there was always plenty in his big leather poke. Barnes recognized to the full the lure of fat packets of big bills laid before a rancher when Barnes quoted the price he would pay for a heard of cow critters. A check was not nearly so effective. So Barnes usually drove a good bargain. He had been plying his lucrative trade in the Brownsville area for years.

Another of Barnes' eccentricities was driving his money-laden buckboard at all times, day or night, whenever he was of a mind to. That eccentricity was modified somewhat by the fact that accompanying him at all times, day and night, when he was on business, were two salty and experienced range riders, one a former Sieber scout, with fast gun-hands.

Still another was reserving a room at the Cattleman's Hotel, thus guaranteeing him a period of rest whenever he felt the need of it.

Payday was past midnight when Barnes rolled into Brownsville. He liked to make deals the day after payday, this expert in psychology. Then the ranchers were relaxed, more receptive, less inclined to argue.

Agosta's stable took care of the horses and the buckboard. Barnes, his gripsack of money under his arm, headed for the Cattleman's Hotel, his two guards in attendance. The lobby clerk greeted him deferentially.

"Your room is all ready, Mr. Barnes," he said. "The same one, second door to the left of the head of the stairs." Barnes thanked him and ascended the stairs, the guards opened the room door, made sure everything was in order.

"Okay," Barnes told them. "Now you can go out and have some fun. Meet you in the lobby around noon."

The guards said goodnight and departed. Barnes placed his money poke beside the head of the bed and composed himself to sleep.

Downstairs, the weary desk clerk half-dozed intermittently as he listened to the din outside, wondering how anybody could really sleep.

Perhaps an hour passed, and a tall, bearded man entered the deserted lobby and made his way to the desk.

"Do you think I can get a room here for the night?" he asked in a low, nicely modulated voice.

"I believe I have one vacant on the third floor," the sleepy clerk replied. "Let me see, now —"

He bent over and scanned the register. It was the last thing he would scan for quite a while. The bearded man's hand flickered down and up, with a gleam of reflecting metal. A gun barrel thudded against the clerk's skull and he fell senseless to the floor.

The tall man slipped around the desk and

dragged the clerk's inert form into the room back of the desk and shut the door. For a moment he stood listening, then ascended the stairs with a noiseless tread.

At the second door to the left of the head of the stairs, he paused, listened again a moment and thrust the thin jaws of a pair of pliers in the keyhole, found the key was in place inside the room.

The pliers gripped the key and slowly turned it until the bolt slid back. The bearded man seized the knob and eased the door open, leaving it open a crack, so that a bar of light filtered from hall lamps through the gloom. He glided toward the bed on which Owen Barnes lay.

Barnes was a light sleeper. His eyes snapped open and he saw the man looming over him. "What —" he began.

Again the slashing gun barrel, and Barnes fell back unconscious; the tall man scooped up the money poke and eased out of the room, closing the door and taking time to turn the key with the pliers and lock it. He sped down the stairs and out, mingling with the whooping throng on the street, nobody paying him any attention.

Another hour or so passed, and two elderly ranchers who'd had enough of payday entered.

"Where the devil's the clerk?" one wondered.

"In the back room, knockin' off a snooze, the chances are," replied his companion. "I'll have a look."

He passed around the desk, opened the door, and gave a horrified yelp —

"Here he is! All covered with blood! I think he's dead!"

"And my God, look, coming down the stairs!" the other exclaimed.

Lurching down the stairs, his eyes wild, his face streaked with blood, his bare feet weaving and stumbling on the treads, was Owen Barnes.

The ranchers bounded forward and caught him before he fell. Together they eased him into a chair.

"What happened?" one asked.

"Gun-whipped, robbed," Barnes mumbled, sagging against a supporting arm.

The other rancher rushed to the outer door and let loose a volley of yells that quickly brought people into the lobby, exclaiming, bawling questions.

"Fetch Doc Cooper, and sheriff Calder," the rancher shouted above the din. "I think Calder's in the Blue Bell, and Doc oughta be around somewhere, maybe in the Blue Bell, too; he was a while back. Hurry! The desk clerk is mighty bad hurt, maybe killed, I ain't sure."

Men dashed out to care for the chores. Somebody procured water and a towel and the blood was wiped from Barnes' face.

However, he could add nothing to what he had said. He'd been slammed over the head with a gun barrel and when he regained consciousness, his gripsack of money was gone.

Slade and Calder were just debating whether to take a walk in the cool night air when the raving informants burst in and gabbled forth what they knew of the trouble. Both peace officers at once headed for the hotel.

When, without delay, Slade began examining Barnes' injury, another of that gentleman's eccentricities, based on sound common sense, came to light.

"I always wear a night cap, a good, heavy one, when I sleep, to keep my bald head warm," he explained to *El Halcón*. "Wouldn't be surprised if it kept me from being worse hurt."

"It very likely did," replied the Ranger. "The slight cut in your scalp, which bled a good deal, was made by the gun sight. Really, you were little more than badly stunned. There are no indications of fracture that I can ascertain. Nor, I believe, of concussion."

"If he says so, there ain't," the sheriff put in. "Doc Cooper will be the first to tell you so. Here he comes now."

Cooper indeed wasted little more than a glance at Barnes, who was sipping coffee somebody had procured and puffing on a cigarette Slade rolled for him, but at once turned his attention to the desk clerk, who was just beginning to show a return to consciousness. Both he and Slade concluded that the clerk was not as badly hurt as appeared. The doctor administered a stimulant and soon he was sitting up and able to talk coherently, although he had little to tell.

"Yes, the devil who hit me was a big and tall hellion with black whiskers," he replied to a question from Slade. "That's about all I noticed before I started to look at the register and the sky fell in on me."

"But that's enough," Slade remarked to the sheriff as they moved away to give the doctor room to pad and bandage the gash in the clerk's head.

"Figure it was Selby?" Calder murmured.

"Without a doubt," Slade answered. "The master's touch — handled the chore himself, without a slip. And I've a notion he made a good haul."

"You can bet on that," said the sheriff. "Barnes always packs plenty in that old gripsack of his. Looks like the horned toad put one over, all right."

"Yes, he did," Slade agreed. "But I'll admit I don't see how we could possibly have anticipated this one. Had we known Barnes was going to show up packing a hefty sum of money, we might have been able to guard against what happened."

"Nobody ever knows what that old coot is going to do," growled Calder. "Sometimes I think he don't know himself. Wonder where the two jiggers who always ride with him are. I'll ask him."

"I think they are over at Matamoros," Barnes replied to the question. "Had no notion I might need 'em, nothing like this ever happened in the hotel before that I ever heard tell of. And, after all, I can hardly ask 'em to sit up all night keeping watch over me, after a hard day of riding." Which, Slade felt, was obvious.

At that moment the hotel manager arrived, with him a couple of helpers.

"I'll have your room changed, clean sheets and pillows, and straighten it up," he told the buyer. "Very, very sorry for what happened."

"Don't blame yourself for something you

couldn't possibly have figured in advance," Barnes replied magnanimously.

"And I think we'd better emulate his guards' example and cross to Matamoros," Slade said to the sheriff. "Nothing more we can do here, so far as I can see."

"A notion," agreed Calder. "Might run into something interesting over there. Guess Estevan is fit to be hog-tied."

"Yes, he'll be blaming himself for what happened, although he has no reason for doing so. He might have bled to death if he'd stuck around that alley. Or have been jumped by three or four of Selby's hellions, who very likely were nosing around."

The doctor assured them that the patients would be okay, and they left the hotel after saying goodnight to everybody.

The payday bust was still going strong when they reached the street, but not so vigorously. Tired nature was taking its toll, as were the quantities of redeye consumed. The roar had subsided to a raucous screech that Slade thought was more sinister than the former bellowing. Now fierce wranglings were breaking loose. But the deputies, the specials, and the floor men were on the job and so far had managed to stop serious trouble before it really got started. Slade and the sheriff made their way through the lessening crowds with no difficulty.

On the crest of the bridge they paused to gaze down at the turgid waters of the Rio Grande, the river being rather high.

"Some day," Slade observed prophetically, "a hurricane is going to roar in from the Gulf, turn this way, and half of both towns will be under water. Some preparations have been made against such an occurrence, but not enough. Keep it in mind, Tom."

"If it washes away about half of both these blasted pueblos, there won't be much lost," grumbled the sheriff. "Seems to me they get worse all the time." Slade laughed and they strolled down the approach to Matamoros, which was also still celebrating.

Amado had their table ready for them when they entered the cantina. Estevan was occupying a chair at it and was obviously in a bad temper.

Dolores and Amado at once joined them and were regaled with an account of what happened at the Cattleman's Hotel. Dolores expressed heartfelt thankfulness that Slade had not been mixed up in it. Amado nodded his wise old head understandingly. Estevan's humor was evidently not improved, for he muttered things in Yaqui that Slade felt were best not translated in the presence of a lady.

Two more hours passed, and the screech had simmered down to a querulous whine. Amado sounded his last call. Dolores had already changed.

The stupendous Texas dawn was flaring in the east as they crossed the bridge and to Jackson Street. But few Brownsville folks gazed upon its beauty. Brownsville slept!

18

The day following payday was fairly quiet, as was to be expected. Owen Barnes procured another poke of money from the bank and rolled north, accompanied by his two guards. Doc Cooper reported the hotel desk clerk's condition satisfactory. Estevan swore his knifed arm was completely healed and insisted that he not be forced to miss any more fun. Slade and Calder sat in the sheriff's office and discussed matters as they stood at the moment.

"And the devil is well heeled again," the sheriff remarked. "He got plenty last night. I felt sorta stunned when Barnes told me the amount that was in that poke, although I knew he always packs plenty with him. He didn't mind the loss over much — he's rich — but he didn't take kind to being batted over the head with a gun barrel."

"Well, you can hardly blame him for that," Slade replied. "And he was very fortunate in wearing that heavy nightcap. Otherwise he might have been seriously hurt."

"And now what's our move?" Calder asked.

"Right now we are in the same predicament as formerly: we haven't any plan," Slade answered. "But maybe Estevan's *amigos* will dig up something. They have a personal interest in the matter since their boss was knifed; they'll be on their toes."

"I can understand that," nodded the sheriff. "And they're always a big help, plumb dependable."

"And there is one other angle I feel will work for us," Slade said slowly.

"How's that?" Calder asked.

"That the gentleman may be intoxicated by success and grow a bit reckless, thus bringing himself into the open, which so far he certainly has not done," *El Halcón* explained. "So far he has been little more than a shadow weaving in and out among the shadows. Several times I've spotted the man I'm convinced is Selby, but I couldn't prove it, couldn't swear to it. He has always definitely kept in the clear. But I have a hunch that won't continue much longer. Well, we'll see. Keep your fingers crossed and hope for the best."

"I'm playing along with your hunch," said

the sheriff. "Thank Pete you've got one at last, where that sidewinder is concerned. Well, should we amble over to Amado's rumhole and see if Estevan has anything to tell us?"

"A good notion, I guess," Slade replied. "Let's go."

However, Estevan had nothing to tell them, and the same went for the night and the day following. But the next day, business picked up, decidedly.

The sheriff was busy with a lot of paper work and Slade was smoking and gazing out the window at the low-lying sun when Estevan entered, his eyes snapping.

"Less than two hours ago the *ladrone* Selby and two others rode west on the river trail," he said.

"The devil he did!" exclaimed Calder.

"*Si,* my *amigo* watched them out of sight," Estevan returned composedly.

"And what do you figure that means?" the sheriff asked of Slade.

"I would say," *El Halcón* answered, "that the gent is on business bent."

"Going to follow them?"

"Would be useless," Slade replied. "We have no idea where they are headed for. We'll just have to sit tight and await developments."

225

The sheriff swore wearily and turned back to his work. Slade smothered his cigarette butt, sat silent for a moment, then said,

"I think I'll mosey over to the Blue Bell for a word with Boyer; he may have heard something. Keep your boys on the watch, Estevan, the devils may circle back to town like they did once before."

"That I will do," the knife man promised and glided out.

When Slade reached the Blue Bell, Boyer did have something to tell him. The saloon-keeper appeared to be in a jubilant mood.

"Remember when we made the deal with Mr. Dunn, you said we still had plenty of land for a herd of cow critters?" he said. "Sefton and I decided getting in the cattle business wouldn't be bad. So we've been dickering with old Zeke Combs who, as you know, is about the biggest rancher in the section. He has a notion to replace his longhorns with the improved stock he's been hearing about and is selling us a big herd at a bargain. Sefton went to the bank and drew out a poke of money about an hour back, and is riding up to Combs' casa to close the deal."

"You mean he's packing cash?" Slade asked.

"That's right," Boyer replied. "Combs

asked for cash."

"God in Heaven!" Slade exclaimed. "Will they never learn?" He was through the swinging doors before the astonished Boyer could ask him what he meant.

Slade raced to Agosto's stable and threw the rig on Shadow. Five minutes later the big black was speeding west on the river trail.

"And once again it looks like it's up to you to keep a good man from dying," Slade told him. Shadow snorted understanding and increased his already flying pace a little.

Slade constantly peered ahead, though with little hope of overtaking Sefton before he turned north on the track that led to Combs' casa, where the lawyer's real danger would begin.

The little towns fell behind. They reached the point where the track leading to the casa joined the main trail, and Slade turned Shadow's nose north. Anxiously he scanned the prairie, hoping against hope he would sight Sefton on the open plain south of the thickets and stands of chaparral that broke the level surface. He saw nothing other than groups of grazing cattle. He spoke to the horse and Shadow extended himself still a trifle more. The big horse was giving his all, and Slade fervently hoped it would be enough. His anxiety increased as he neared the straggles of growth and his ears attuned to the sound he dreaded to hear, the crackle of gunfire that would announce the success of Selby's devilish scheme and death for Vibart Sefton.

The miles flowed back, the stands of brush drew nearer. The racing horse swerved around one and Slade saw, no great distance ahead, Sefton riding at a good pace.

And he saw something else. Over a tall and dense thicket some five hundred yards in front of where Sefton rode, a bird was swooping and darting. Might mean nothing, but it could mean everything, for Sefton would pass close to the bristle of brush, close enough to offer a perfect target for the outlaws, were they really holed up in the thicket awaiting their intended victim, and Slade believed they were.

He again spoke to Shadow, urgently, and the great horse, his nostrils flaring, his eyes gorged with blood, put forth a final burst of speed, sweeping past where the lawyer rode, with the ominous thicket some five hundred yards ahead. Slade whipped his big Winchester from the saddle boot and sprayed the thicket with lead.

The tops of the bushes were violently agitated, and from the thick tangle bulged three horsemen, guns blazing. Bullets buzzed past *El Halcón* like angry hornets. He resolved to take a desperate gamble. Curbing Shadow a little, he reeled in the saddle, lurched forward, and slid to the ground, almost hidden in the tall grass.

The outlaws, one tall, bearded, cut loose whoops of triumph as they saw him fall. What they didn't note was that as he went down, he held on to the long-range rifle.

Flat on the ground, *El Halcón* clamped the rifle to his shoulder, glanced along the sights. The big Winchester boomed sullenly and one of the outlaws whirled from the saddle to lie motionless. Answering bullets whipped past the prostrate Ranger, one ripping the sleeve of his shirt. A slight shift of the rifle muzzle, another burst of flame, and there were two riderless horses galloping across the prairie.

But the bearded man charged straight ahead, his gun flaming. Another slight shift of the black muzzle. Slade, taking a frightful chance, tried to drill him through the shoulder, for he earnestly desired to take Selby alive. But just as he squeezed the trigger, Selby lurched sideways and the slug caught him dead center. He rose in his stirrups, lurched forward and slid to the ground, to lie writhing, a last bullet from his gun fanning *El Halcón*'s face as the weapon dropped from his nerveless hand.

Warily, Slade got to his feet, rifle ready for instant action. But a glance told him there was nothing to fear from Selby's two followers. He walked to where Selby lay, his false beard dangling grotesquely from one ear, and gazed into the face of the dying outlaw leader. Selby glared up at him and tried to speak, but choked on the blood welling in his throat. Slade held the star of the Rangers before his glazing eyes.

The symbol of law and justice was the last thing Mostyn Selby saw on this earth.

With a sigh, Slade replaced the badge in its pocket and for another moment gazed down regretfully at the dead face of the able man who might have gone far had he not for some reason taken the wrong fork of the trail.

Vibart Sefton was riding toward him, shouting amazed questions. Slade answered them, briefly, for abruptly he was very tired. Sefton stared at the dead outlaws.

"And it would seem that, in addition to all else, I owe you my life," he said heavily.

"Thank Shadow, my horse," Slade replied. "It is due to his speed and endurance you are alive. As it is, you can go ahead and close your deal with Combs. And you might do me one favor."

"I'd be a nice one to refuse you anything," Sefton retorted. "What is it?"

"Don't ever again go riding around alone and packing a lot of money."

"I won't," the lawyer promised whole-heartedly.

"What about those?" he asked, gesturing to the bodies.

"I desire they be left just as they are until the sheriff can look them over," Slade answered. "He'll ride up and fetch them to town. You might tell Combs to have some of his boys round up the horses and remove the rigs."

"Mostyn Selby!" Sefton exclaimed. "The last person I would have thought of being mixed up in something off-color."

"You have plenty of company where that is concerned," Slade said. "He had quite a few folks fooled. Too many of his brand, able, adroit, with a touch of genius, but lacking the little something that goes for the making of honesty and square dealing. Well, so wags the world. Be seeing you."

Slade let Shadow choose his own gait on the way to town, and by the time they reached Brownsville, not long after full dark, the big black was rarin' to go.

Sheriff Calder shook his head and swore

when Slade gave him an account of his ruckus with the outlaw band.

"Yes, Selby didn't lack courage," the Ranger concluded. "Game to the last, and hard. His dying shot came very nearly getting me. Guess it'll be up to you and the Commissioners to dispose of his property. Might be a good notion to turn it over to the Albemarle workers. They, of course, were not a part of his owlhoot following; he was too smart for that. They may have wondered about his frequent absences, but he was a good man to work for and naturally they didn't ask any questions."

"I'll commandeer Agosto the stablekeeper's light wagon in the morning and fetch in the carcasses," Calder said, "Reckon they'll be the last floor decorations for a while, with you riding off."

"Not for a few days," Slade replied. "Well, I'm going over to the Blue Bell and knock off a bite to eat. Then to the cantina to make peace with Estevan, who is going to be very much put out at missing the fun."

"And say goodbye to Dolores, eh?"

"After a fashion," Slade smiled.

Three days later, when Dolores watched him ride away to where duty called and new adventure waited, tall and graceful atop his great black horse, the morning sunlight

232

etching his sternly handsome profile in flame, her farewell, if one might call it that, consisted of just three words —

"I'll be waiting!"

We hope you have enjoyed this Large Print book. Other Thorndike, Wheeler, Kennebec, and Chivers Press Large Print books are available at your library or directly from the publishers.

For information about current and upcoming titles, please call or write, without obligation, to:

Publisher
Thorndike Press
295 Kennedy Memorial Drive
Waterville, ME 04901
Tel. (800) 223-1244

or visit our Web site at:

http://gale.cengage.com/thorndike

OR

Chivers Large Print
published by AudioGO Ltd
St James House, The Square
Lower Bristol Road
Bath BA2 3SB
England
Tel. +44(0) 800 136919
www.audiogo.co.uk

All our Large Print titles are designed for easy reading, and all our books are made to last.